AMETHYST FLAME

Amethyst Flame: The Flame Series - Book 2

By Caris Roane

Copyright © 2016 Twin Bridges Creations LLC

Formatting and cover by Bella Media Management.

ISBN-13: 978-1530193059

AMETHYST FLAME

The Flame Series - Book 2

Caris Roane

Dear Reader,

Welcome to the second installment of the Flame Series called
AMETHYST FLAME!

**In this story, Vaughn, a powerful vampire serving as a Border
Patrol officer for his corrupt world, falls for a dangerous witch who
alone is the key to saving his long lost sister...**

Vampire Officer Vaughn of the Crescent Border Patrol gets called
to a triple homicide in a deadly place called the Graveyard. When he
finds that Emma Delacey has been summoned to the same crime scene,
warning bells sound. He's tried to suppress his desire for the beautiful
witch knowing nothing good can come of a relationship in the alter
world of Five Bridges. But her auburn hair and glittering green eyes call
to him as no woman has since he became an alter vampire. As an evil
wizard hounds them both, Vaughn must come to terms with his deepest
fears especially when Emma proves to be the key to saving his sister
from a madman's torture.

I hope you're enjoying the Flame Series. If you've missed the first
book, BLOOD FLAME, you can find lots of info *here* (http://www.
carisroane.com/blood-flame/).

I've had a wonderful time developing a world inspired by my love for
bridges and of course, hunky warrior vampire types!

Enjoy!

Caris Roane

CHAPTER ONE

W e didn't save them after all."
Vaughn heard the break in Emma Delacey's voice. His own chest was damn tight and his throat hurt.

He stood beside her at the top of a deep ditch in the middle of the area of Five Bridges known as the Graveyard. Bodies were dumped here every night to be cleaned up by a designated Tribunal squad in the early morning hours.

Tonight was no exception.

He moved closer to her, blood pounding in his head. He stared down at the bodies of three familiar teenage girls, triplets in fact. Two months ago, he and Emma had rescued the girls from a despicable human trafficking organization. Now they were here, naked, beat-up, and laid out like discarded mannequins. Their arms and legs were at odd angles, bones fractured.

The bastard who'd abducted them hadn't just killed them, he'd tortured each one.

"Jesus. They've been savaged." Vaughn found it hard to breathe, but he wasn't sure if it was grief or blind rage. He couldn't believe the girls had been kidnapped a second time.

Emma moaned softly like a wounded animal. She'd become a good friend in recent weeks, despite the fact she was an *alter* witch and his natural enemy. He slid an arm around her shoulders.

She didn't pull away, either. "How did Wizard Loghry find them

1

again? I thought they were safe. Their parents said they'd take them out of state."

"Maybe they did. But you know what Loghry is. He has massive connections throughout the Southwest. He could have hired dozens of people to hunt them down and bring them back."

"He must have done this for revenge."

"I have no doubt about that."

Emma shook her head slowly, her fingers on her lips. "Maybe if we'd left them alone, they'd still be alive."

"You don't know that, Em. Girls like these are trapped inside Loghry's sex clubs with no way to escape. They get used up and after a time no one sees them again."

She took a shuddering breath. "I've never felt so sick about being in Five Bridges."

He got where Emma was coming from. Having saved the girls the first time, she'd believed they'd done some good. To have these beautiful girls abducted again added to his hatred of the world they'd each gotten stuck in.

But there was another issue they had to deal with, a critical one, as in why he and Emma had been summoned to the scene. He patrolled almost exclusively in Crescent and he knew Emma rarely worked this part of Five Bridges. It felt like a set-up.

His suspicions grew as another SUV pulled up. There was no reason to have this many officers at a Graveyard homicide scene.

He recognized the vehicle as belonging to the Elegance Border Patrol and he slid his arm from Emma's shoulders. He didn't want her to become a target because she'd been fraternizing with a vampire.

Vaughn recognized the officer in the police cruiser, a warlock he despised. His nostrils flared. He'd as soon kill the man as get near him.

There was no love lost among the five different territory Border Patrols. But he loathed those men and women on the take no matter which species. The warlock, who stayed in his vehicle with his com to his mouth, was in deep with the three cartels that ruled the underworld of Five Bridges. So, who was he reporting back to?

Probably Donaldson at the Trib or maybe the corrupt chief at the Elegance station.

Vaughn became acutely aware he'd left his half-sword in his SUV. Easton had pushed him to get out here fast and to keep a low profile. He didn't want shots fired in the Graveyard. And he definitely didn't want Vaughn battling any Elegance officers who might show up. Vaughn was to leave his weapons in his SUV, head to the crime scene, take a quick look, then report back to Crescent. Get in, get out.

Despite Easton's orders, Vaughn had his Glock with him.

Vaughn reverted his attention to the crime scene and started looking for anything out of place that might indicate a bomb. But it was hard to tell. The whole massive central area of the *alter* world, known as the Graveyard, looked like a war zone made worse by an explosion a month ago. Dirt, rocks and cement had been flung all over the surrounding ditches and at least a dozen small bridges that crossed them.

He spoke quietly. "We're in trouble here, Em." He'd started abbreviating her name a few phone calls ago. They were good friends now. They were at least that, though they could have been a lot more. In another life, they could have been everything.

Emma turned toward him and kept her voice low as well. "I know. Loghry's hand is all over this. But Vaughn, even though we agreed never to see each other again, I'm so glad you're here. I can't tell you how much I've valued all our conversations since that first night. In fact, the only reason I think I can bear what Loghry has done to these girls is because you're beside me."

He felt the same way and resisted a powerful impulse to haul her into his arms and hold her.

His relationship with Emma had grown complicated since the night of the rescue. Afterward, they'd gone to a bar, one of the few that served all five *alter* species. He'd ordered a couple of beers, then another matched set.

By the time six bottles were sitting on the table, he knew he was in trouble. He'd walked her outside, then drawn her into the shadows and kissed her. When he'd suggested they go to his house, she hadn't hesitated. Neither had she minded flying for the first time with a vampire.

The sex that had followed had been hot as hell though he couldn't believe he'd crossed the line. Vampires and witches didn't date.

Afterward, they'd agreed not to see each other again, but the phone had been a different case. He'd talked with Emma almost every night since. He'd call her after their respective shifts and a lot of those conversations had gone well past dawn. But this was the first time he'd seen her since the rescue. Despite the fact that she was a witch, the enemy of his kind, he couldn't deny his powerful attraction to her or that he'd come to care about her as much as he did.

Tears shimmered in her green eyes, which made her even more beautiful than he remembered. She had thick auburn hair, the front portion pulled into her usual top knot. The rest hung almost to her waist. Her creamy complexion glowed in the moonlight and her snug jeans and t-shirt reminded him of everything he'd once held in his arms.

The pain she obviously felt about the deaths below echoed his own. Doing good in their sick, corrupt world was a rare thing, and he hated that their joint efforts to save these teens two months ago had ended in tragedy. But he had to give Emma this, she had grit and he loved that about her.

As for the author of the crime, Wizard Loghry was one of the most vicious criminals in Five Bridges. The amethyst flame addicted warlock had strong ties to the cartels that ruled the underworld of their *alter* society, which meant he was well-protected. He could do whatever he wanted without fear of repercussion.

He operated several sex clubs in Elegance Territory stocked primarily with teenage girls. He systematically abducted them from the human part of Arizona, then smuggled them past the border that separated the city of Phoenix from the cordoned off province of Five Bridges.

Sometimes the girls entered Loghry's work establishments in their fragile human forms. Other times, he put them through the difficult *alter* process and made vampires out of them. It was rumored he liked fangs in his throat, and that he'd kept a female vampire imprisoned for years in the labyrinth below his Elegance mansion.

Emma crossed her arms protectively over her chest. "Did your boss send you out here?"

"Yep. Easton delivered his orders personally." Chief Easton, of the Crescent Territory Border Patrol, had taken pains to make sure Vaughn made it to the Graveyard. Alone.

Emma snorted her disgust. "Donaldson came to my office himself and he never does that."

Vaughn heard several male voices. Turning, he saw that three more Elegance Border Patrol officers had arrived and were laughing it up near the first SUV.

Vaughn jerked his chin toward them. "Any of those warlocks clean?" He was pretty sure he knew the answer, but he asked anyway.

She turned to glance in the direction of her territory's policing force. "No. Just ignore them. They're vermin."

He shifted his gaze back to her. He knew she didn't take bribes. Neither did he. Being on the take had a stench, and he could smell a corrupt officer at a hundred yards.

Over the beers he and Emma had shared the night of the rescue, she'd told him she was clean but that half the Elegance force wasn't. He'd confessed a similar statistic for his own vampire territory of Crescent. That's when things had shifted and he'd started seeing her as a woman he admired as opposed to a witch who could kill him with the energy she could release through the tips of her fingers.

Another burst of laughter came on the heels of the arrival of yet another Border Patrol vehicle. His survival instincts kicked in. "We should leave, Em. Right now. I can fly us straight out of here. Someone else can pick up your bike and my SUV later."

He held out his arm to her and gestured to his foot. He'd flown her before, so she knew the drill. All she had to do was hop on and he'd have them out of danger within seconds.

She glanced at his boot but shook her head. "I can't go. Not yet."

"Why? We both know this is a set-up, and isn't it bad enough Loghry got these girls? So, how about we get the hell out of here?"

"Vaughn, you know what this is like for me. It's the way my *alter* power manifests. I have to tend to the girls. Their spirits are calling to me." She started down the side of the ditch.

Vaughn's heartrate kicked up a notch. "Emma, don't do this. We've gotta go now."

"The girls need me and it's the least I can do after what they've been through."

Vaughn didn't try to argue with her and instead began his own descent. He might not want her to stay, but like hell he was leaving her alone in No Man's Land.

~ ~ ~

Emma Delacey, Tribunal Public Safety officer, understood Vaughn's concern. She felt it as well, that she was heading into a trap.

She'd been the first to arrive at the triple homicide in the Graveyard, a part of Five Bridges she'd only been to a handful of times.

Her corrupt boss, Tribunal Chief Donaldson, had ordered her to head out here or resign. She wasn't a quitter, though the sweat on his forehead had told her she was in trouble the minute he'd come into her office. The three major cartels of Five Bridges owned one of Donaldson's testicles. The dark spellcasters of Elegance territory held the other in a crushing grip. She wasn't even sure she blamed Donaldson anymore. If you were high up in the administration and didn't play ball, you got killed.

She picked her way carefully down the side of the ditch, avoiding chunks of blown-up cement, cactus and a helluvalot of rocks.

Her *alter* witch senses told her the girls had died within the past two hours. She also knew because of her unique gift that the ghosts were struggling to leave their bodies.

She didn't know why her witchness leaned toward the deceased. But it had from the time she'd gotten stuck with the spellcaster gene and sentenced to live out her life in Five Bridges. She'd been here seven years and had strived to remain as human as possible by repressing her gifts.

Yet, the sight of the teens below made her wish she'd taken a different course. If she'd spent her nights developing her abilities, instead of ignoring them, maybe she'd be able to take Loghry on. But he was one of the most powerful spellcasters in Elegance and she was an infant by comparison.

Anger bloomed in her chest suddenly as she stared down at the young women. They would never breathe again, never fall in love and marry, never bear children. And all because of a psychopathic wizard who ran a vile sex racket that exploited teens.

Everyone knew who Loghry was, as well as the extent of his operation in Elegance. He didn't go out in public often, being one of the rare monsters who lived a secluded life. She'd only seen him once herself a year ago. It had been July in the desert and despite the intense summer heat, he'd worn a black scarf around his neck, no doubt to hide the violet markings on his throat. An addiction to any of the flame drugs created a skin discoloration in the shape of flames, especially on the neck, sometimes rising onto the face.

When the pull of the girls' struggle became an ache in Emma's chest, she came to a decision. She would embrace what she'd avoided for so long. Simple witch spells or standard police work weren't effective against Loghry and his kind. She needed power, the kind that came from being a fully engaged *alter* witch. From this moment forward, she meant to acquire as much power as she could.

She turned to Vaughn, who had made his way into the ditch as well and stood beside her once more. "Loghry is not going to win this time. I won't let him."

"What do you mean?"

"I mean that I'm not going to hold back anymore. I'm going to access who I am in this shitfest of a world. I should have done it years ago. Maybe if I had, these young women would still be alive."

"Em, please don't. You're talking about a level of power the dark witches employ. I've felt how much potential you have. Besides, I know what this means to you. I know how hard you've tried to hold onto your humanity."

Emma's heart heated up as she stared back at Vaughn. Was it possible he felt more for her than she thought? They'd had an amazing round of sex in his townhouse, but they'd also agreed not to repeat anything like it again.

Then, of course, he'd called her and they'd fallen into conversation like they'd always known each other. She'd come to cherish their time on the phone like a lifeline she'd grabbed in high seas. "Thanks for saying as much. It means a lot. All this time, I've held back developing my gifts for selfish reasons. I've been trying to hold onto something that doesn't exist anymore, that hasn't existed from the time I was slipped the *alter* witch serum. And I owe it to these girls to make a change.

"If I can become a force that will bring Loghry down, then I don't care about anything else. Not after tonight. I'm done trying to use a rolled up newspaper to battle a hurricane."

From the rim of the ditch above, one of the officers made a crack about 'bloodsuckers', the slur aimed at Vaughn.

She glanced up, surprised to see seven officers now, standing side-by-side and watching them. "Bastards. All those men are on the take."

"Just ignore them." He sounded angry.

She met his gaze once more. "I'm going to fight Loghry on his own terms. There's no other way to do this. So, please don't interfere."

"And there's nothing I can say?"

"I'm afraid not."

For a moment, though, time slowed as she looked at Vaughn. She'd wanted to see him again so badly after she'd been with him the night of the rescue.

He was an incredibly handsome man, rugged looking with his thick black hair cropped close on the sides and tattoos showing through on his skin. He had straight black brows, drawn tight together in concern and gray eyes that melted her into a puddle. His cheeks were strong and angled to a firm jaw. His lips were full and sensual and had stolen her last reservation when he'd kissed her outside the bar.

Having sex with him had been an incredible, healing experience.

Yet now she was here.

She gave herself a mental shake and turned back to the girls. She didn't wait for Vaughn to say anything else. Instead, she extended her arms slightly and held her hands palms up.

As she'd never done before, she opened herself up to her spellcaster power. She focused her energy and thoughts on the core of her being, on all that she was as an *alter* witch.

A sensation like electricity whipped through her, awakening her latent abilities. To her surprise, she found the seat of her power with no trouble at all. And contrary to all expectation, everything about the moment felt sacred and good, not corrupt like she'd feared.

After that, two things happened simultaneously. Odd snapshots started floating though her mind, images of the Graveyard, the ditch, the dead girls and Vaughn. She knew she was looking at pieces of the immediate future. Because the pictures held a serious warning, they were an equal pull on her attention. But the girls needed her help desperately. If they were unable to leave their bodies, they could get stuck forever right here in the Graveyard.

She turned her attention to them and directed her whirling witch energy toward the triplets. Power flowed and swirled above the girls until she could feel each one, their fears and sadness, even their confusion. Mentally, she began to coax them to let go of their time on earth and to leave their bodies. It wasn't long before the air in the ditch began to shimmer and shortly afterward the ghosts rose into the air.

They appeared dazed at first. They looked at one another then Emma and finally at Vaughn. Each tried to talk, but couldn't.

Emma stood amazed by how they appeared. She'd seen ghosts before, but only as fleeting wisps of smoky air.

Not this time. Each was fully formed as though possessing a body, yet not quite a body. It almost seemed as though the girls were working on taking shape. She wondered if Vaughn could see them, but one glance told her he didn't.

They seemed to be communicating with each other and a moment later bits of clothing appeared, though more like smoke than real fabric. Colors as well. The center girl, who had the strongest personality, now wore a red tank top, blue jeans and running shoes.

The one to the right donned red shorts, a dark blue crop top and navy sandals with flowers at the top of the t-strap. While the third wore a red plaid short dress, dark stockings and black Mary-Jane shoes. The girls seemed to like red.

They were lovely, each with long, curly, light brown hair and large, blue eyes.

The blue-jeans ghost drew close to Emma, then addressed her telepathically. *You saved us once. I remember now. You, and this man, took us home the night we were abducted the first time.*

The ghostly voice in Emma's head made her feel dizzy, but she responded immediately. *We did. It was the finest night of my life since becoming an* alter *witch.*

Oh, you're a witch. She shifted to look at Vaughn. *But this man can't see me, can he?*

I don't think so. And in case you're wondering, Officer Vaughn is a vampire.

The ghost swept backward, rejoining her sisters. But she continued to talk with Emma. *There was a lot of pain from what that madman was doing to us and he ordered vampires to take our blood. I think maybe the vampires were the ones who killed us. I remember getting weaker and weaker. And now we're here.*

By the pallor of their skin, Emma knew she was right. Once more, a terrible grief assailed her that these young women had been robbed of their lives. Yet, it cemented her determination to do what she could to prevent Loghry from continuing his abduction of innocent teens.

The girls, almost as one, shifted their attention upward to the ditch ridge. Emma started to turn to see what they were looking at, but suddenly the three spirits flew around both her and Vaughn. They cried out in loud voices, almost wailing.

The one with the blue jeans got in front of Emma and tried to speak, but no words formed. She seemed really distressed.

Emma attempted to make telepathic contact with her, but only static returned.

The wailing grew louder until Emma finally had to cover her ears. She didn't understand what was wrong.

~ ~ ~

Vaughn had never felt so much power emanate from Emma before as though she'd opened the floodgates. Maybe she had. He had an impression of the three ghosts but nothing more than that, though a bad feeling crawled through him like a snake. Something wasn't right.

Emma was bent over as if in pain, her hands held to her ears.

He felt a strange sensation on his face, like soft fingers dragging over his skin. Had to be the ghosts attempting to communicate with him. The message felt like a warning.

He turned to glance back up at the top of the ditch, wondering if the Elegance officers intended to fire on them. "Shit." There were no longer seven but at least twelve Elegance witches and warlocks staring down at him, all members of the territory's Border Patrol.

The fingers on his face moved swiftly now and his instincts vibrated heavily, sending warning after warning through his mind.

A second passed.

Then another.

But the moment he watched all those Border Patrol hands move in the direction of their firearms, he reacted swiftly. He didn't have time to warn Emma. Instead, he grabbed her around the waist and as fast as he could, he hauled her straight up into the night sky.

The firing began at almost the same time.

He whipped through the air and kept flying. He didn't shift course either, just headed higher and higher out of the line of what became a barrage of pistol fire.

He only slowed down when he couldn't hear a single distant pop.

Hovering in the air, he reached for Emma telepathically. *Emma! Are you okay? Are you hit?*

I don't know. I don't think so. But I can hardly breathe. I think you might be holding me too tight.

Sorry. He released his death grip on her waist, though he still kept her pressed firmly against him. He doubted she could levitate. Some of the more powerful witches and warlocks could. But until tonight, Emma had kept the brakes on her power, so she probably couldn't.

"We're pretty high up, aren't we?"

He cleared his mind and became aware she was shaking head to foot. She'd only flown one time before with him, but that had been two months ago.

Still holding her in a firm clasp, he told her to plant her feet on his right boot. He eased her down a little until she connected. When she did, he felt her relax right away.

"That helps so much." As she slid an arm around his neck, she glanced around. "How high would you say we are?"

"About half a mile."

"Oh, my God. But what happened? What was that back there and how did you think to move us so fast?"

Vaughn told her the exact sequence. "When you were doubled over, I felt fingers on my face. It was the girls, right?"

"Yes, they'd just left their bodies. They were flying around us, shrieking so loud I could hardly stand it. Didn't you hear them?"

"No, but I could sense a warning in their touch. That's when I gabbed you."

"The gunfire was deafening. I take it all seven officers were firing."

"Not seven. There were at least twelve."

Emma groaned. "Then Loghry really wanted us dead."

"No question. It also means he won't quit until we are."

Adrenaline had his nerves on edge. He needed to take her somewhere, but if Loghry was after them, where could they go to be safe?

He gathered up his vampire shielding ability and let it flow.

"What is that?" Emma turned slightly in his arms.

"The only defense I have against you spellcasters."

"Your vampire ability to disguise yourself?"

"Exactly. You okay with that?"

An odd chuckle escaped her throat. "My kind just tried to kill me. So yeah, I'm okay with whatever you need to do."

"Well, right now, I'm trying to figure out where we should go. My townhouse won't be safe. Not now. Maybe never, after tonight. But what about your home in Elegance? I know you told me you have a powerful security-spell over the entire property."

"I do. And I'm sure we would be safe there."

~ ~ ~

As Vaughn turned toward the east and began to fly her in the direction of Elegance Territory, Emma asked him to go slow. Not because she was afraid, but because she'd never seen this part of Five Bridges from high overhead before.

Her right leg was bothering her a little. Maybe one of the bullets had nicked her, but it probably wasn't anything serious. She'd have a look when she got home.

He kept them moving steadily east, toward Elegance and even began a slow descent so she could see the land better.

Five Bridges had over a hundred small bridges linking up the pitted landscape. Long ditches crisscrossed the land as part of a containment solution to the drug and human trafficking problem that had been a result of the flame revolution. Those ditches, thousands of them, were almost impossible to traverse. Yet, dozens of runners, loaded with flame drugs, tried night after night to get to the human world beyond the barrier of barbed wire. Too many succeeded, though a large number died in the process.

Underground tunnels also riddled the area beneath Five Bridges, each opening onto a human home in Phoenix where more drugs and unconscious humans were carted back and forth. Corruption was rampant in the province and because of the amount of money involved, pay-offs went to some of the highest levels in Phoenix government.

The result? Two ghosts now flew alongside Vaughn and the third next to Emma.

She could see the dense stretch of barbed wire as Vaughn crossed the border from the Graveyard into Elegance.

She felt funny, though, and her right calf was sore, like it was bruised. Maybe a bullet had kicked a rock up as Vaughn had carried her into the air. She also felt a little lightheaded, but it wouldn't be long before she was home.

Another minute, and she could see her house. "It's the third on the right, but go to the side yard. There, just past the tree."

He dropped down slowly until he was on the sidewalk. She stepped off his boot, but because this was only the second time she'd flown with him, she took a moment to regain her balance.

And her leg really hurt.

She reached the door, pulled it open and without thinking went inside. She'd completely forgotten the nature of the spell until Vaughn shouted, "Emma, what the fuck is going on?"

~ ~ ~

Vaughn couldn't see anything but the side of the house, no doors, no windows, which was bad all by itself. But Emma had moved toward the wall, then disappeared.

He drew his Glock and bent his knees. "Emma? Are you all right?"

Suddenly, she reappeared in front of him. "Sorry, Vaughn. I wasn't thinking." She winced slightly and rubbed her forehead. "Come on. I'll lead you in."

Vaughn nodded, but he was pissed. He hated the feeling of being shut out and unable to properly assess a situation because of a spell.

Slowly, he holstered his Glock.

Emma took his hand. "I can tell this is bugging you. But the spell only covers the exterior of the property. You'll see."

Before he'd taken two steps, however, he tugged on her hand once more and drew her to a stop. "Is this some kind of witchy thing? Are you enthralling me?"

Her auburn brows rose. "I don't know what you mean."

He lifted their joined hands. "This? What I'm feeling, like a soft flow of electricity working its way up my arm."

At that, she looked away from him and a blush suffused her cheeks. It took him a moment before he realized she was embarrassed. "Did you put a spell on me?"

She shook her head and finally looked up at him again. She swallowed once. "It's something very human, I'm afraid, but probably enhanced by my witchness in a way I don't yet understand." She drew closer and lowered her voice. "Do you remember the night we were together? In your townhouse?"

Did he remember? He'd replayed it in his mind about a thousand times. Two months had passed, but it was as fresh as though it had happened about five seconds ago. "Of course I remember."

"Well, the same thing happened back then, like this hum of electricity between us. I think being with you awakened something inside me."

"You're saying your witch is attracted to me?"

"Something like that." Using her other hand, she waved it over him. "What woman, in her right mind, wouldn't be? I mean look at you."

Given the situation, he was stunned that desire for Emma cascaded over him in a quick hot wave. He squeezed her hand. "I've thought about our time together, Em, a lot, wishing we could be together again."

"I know. Me, too." Emma squeezed his hand in return. He could see a sheen of sweat on her forehead and she was looking unusually pale.

"Yet, there's no real future for us, together, I mean." Yet, here he was, on the threshold of entering her home, a place he'd never thought he'd be.

She nodded, then turned toward the house, still nothing but a solid wall to him.

When she began to disappear again, he tugged on her hand. "Hey, go slow here. All I'm seeing is a wall."

She smiled back at him. "You'll be okay."

As he drew within a foot of the house and probably because he held Emma's hand, the doorway finally revealed itself to him and he crossed the threshold.

But as he entered her home, he noticed she'd started limping. Glancing down, he saw that she was leaving bloody shoe-prints behind. "Emma. Holy shit."

She turned back to him, appearing dazed. "What?"

"You've been shot."

CHAPTER TWO

Emma had been shot a couple of times before, once painfully in the stomach. But as she turned to look back at the tracks of blood, the bruising in her leg suddenly blossomed into a mountain of pain.

Sometimes adrenaline would do that, keep you from getting the full impact until it was safe.

She felt the floor pushing toward her face.

The next moment, strong arms held her tight against a broad chest, then she was airborne.

At first she couldn't figure out what had happened, until she heard Vaughn's voice. "Hang on, Em."

She was in his arms and he was carrying her.

"Bathroom," she called out through a haze of pain.

"Which one?"

"Master." She tried to lift her arm to gesture to the east wing of the house, but her eyes were closed, squinched together, and she couldn't see anything. She felt abominably nauseated.

"It hurts."

"I know. I've got you."

She grabbed his tank, maybe at the shoulder, she wasn't sure. She pulled it into a knot and breathed through a spasm. Her whole leg was on fire.

Cool tile hit her next as he laid her out on the floor near the tub. She felt him tugging at her shoes and cursing a couple of times.

He began easing her pants off. "This is gonna hurt."

"Do it fast."

He swept her pants down her legs. She cried out and turned on her side, struggling to get air in her lungs.

She felt warm hands on her legs. "The bullet went through but you've got a nasty wound. Let me call someone."

She forced her eyes open and caught his forearm. "No. Don't. We can't. There's so much corruption. I don't want anyone to know where we are or that I've been hurt. I just need my stuff. This isn't my first GSW. There's a wicker basket under the sink I made up a while ago."

She lay her head on her arm and swallowed hard. Another wave of nausea hit her because of the pain.

Vaughn opened one of several cupboard doors until he found the basket. He held it up for her to see.

"Just slide it over. Fast."

The basket hurtled toward her. She caught it then reached for the vial first, popped the cork with one hand and guzzled the contents.

The effects of the spelled liquid were immediate, sending a warmth down her throat and into her stomach. A similar sensation sped through her veins. The pain started drifting away.

She closed her eyes, but soon felt soft fingers dragging over her face. Ah, the girls were here.

"You're smiling." Vaughn's gorgeous, deep voice again. "Was that an opiate?"

She chuckled. "No. It's my own concoction with a spell. It's made from flowers from my garden. I think one of them is used in amethyst flame. No wonder Loghry's addicted."

When the first rush of feel-good passed, she tapped the basket. "There's a jar in there with a lavender colored balm. All I need you to do is spread some on the wound. Can you do that?"

"Of course."

"Am I still bleeding?"

"Not as bad."

"Good. The balm will take care of the rest."

She closed her eyes again. She could feel the ghosts flying around the room. They seemed almost cheerful. They were probably getting used to their new state.

Just like she was. She chuckled again. "I'm so smart." Had she said that aloud?

She felt a pressure on her calf that only registered as pain in the dimmest way. "Put it on thick. You know, glob it on."

"Will do." Then, "Jesus." He sounded startled.

"What?"

"It's healing so fast."

"Yeah, cuz I'm smart." She laughed again. Everything seemed so funny right now, including her self-proclamations of genius.

"Well, you're definitely smart, although I'd say you're also high as a kite."

She worked to open her eyes. "I should have shared." She lifted her hand that still held the vial. "You can have the few drops at the bottom."

Vaughn's face was suddenly hovering above hers. "I'll pass." But he took the vial from her anyway. Probably a good idea. It was made of glass and her motor functions were off.

"Vaughn?"

"Yes?"

He was still right there above her. "You are so beautiful. I mean, I know I should say 'handsome', but oh, my God, your eyes are like steel and your face has all these angled planes. And I love your straight black brows because it makes you look serious and committed. I like committed men." She chuckled some more. "Like Loghry. That bastard is damn committed."

She saw Vaughn's lips curve. Then his face left her line of sight. She reached for his tank, wanting to pull him back, but her arm wasn't working right. "Where are you going?"

"Nowhere. I'm right here."

When he floated back into her field of vision, this time she made a concerted effort to grab his shirt. She succeeded and pulled him closer. "Vaughn, I want you. I've wanted you bad since you took me on your couch. Do you know that I started volunteering for any Trib assignment that would take me to Crescent? I wanted to see your face again. Your body. Oh, God, your body. You are so built. Did I ever tell you that?"

She tried to pull him down to her, but he gently took her hand and unwrapped it from around his shirt. "You're drugged out, sweetheart."

"But I know what I'm saying. I want you." What she didn't know was *why* she was pelting him with her lust. "Sorry. You're right. I'm not myself."

"It's okay. I have a confession to make as well. I've spied on you. I'd make any excuse to go to the Trib. I saw you a few times."

She laughed. Everything seemed so funny. "I love that you've been watching me. Now I don't feel like such a dork. Maybe we're both dorks."

"Maybe we are." Was he chuckling as well?

"You're not. I am, but you're not. You're a man. A real man. I respect the hell out of you, Vaughn. I need you to know that, even if my head is swimming right now."

She remembered that something else needed doing. "Wrap up my leg with that other thing." Her hand flopped as though all on its own toward the basket.

Her mind flowed in and out now, but she could feel him working on her leg.

The next thing she knew she was falling into something soft. Oh, her bed. Not falling. Vaughn was settling her on the sheets. She turned on her side and slid her hands beneath her cheek. Warmth flowed over her. Maybe he'd covered her up.

Once more, she felt lovely soft fingers on her face.

"Vaughn?"

"Sleep for a bit."

"I will."

Then she was gone.

~ ~ ~

Once Emma drifted off, Vaughn headed to the bathroom. He put the basket back where he'd found it, then cleaned up the blood from the floor all the way to the distant side door.

With Emma out cold because of her gunshot wound concoction, he needed to take care of his own issue. He hadn't gotten hurt, but Emma's blood had gotten on his leathers and his boots. He didn't have a pleasant smell, either, something like fear and death combined with a whole lot of lust thrown into the mix.

She'd said she wanted him bad. He felt the same way about her and it hadn't helped to take her pants off and see a sheer-as-hell violet thong barely covering her sex.

He removed his Glock and holster, setting it on the bathroom sink. He then stripped out of his clothes and stepped into the oversized shower. It felt good to soap up and rinse off.

Something had changed for him in the past hour since he'd taken care of Emma then put her to bed. It had all felt so normal, like they were a couple, and it had left him feeling shaky. Or hell, maybe it was the adrenaline.

He didn't get what was going on with him because he usually didn't give a shit whether he lived or died.

Yet right now he did.

As he shut the water off, he pulled a towel from the nearby bar and dried his hair. Wiping down his body, he glanced at his cock. Here was the main problem. The damn thing was half-swollen with desire for the woman lying partially clothed in her bed.

When she'd downed the vial of her witch-remedy pain-killer and began healing at lightning speed, he'd started to relax. Her wound and all the blood that had soaked her jeans had driven straight through his heart. He didn't want her hurt, and he really didn't want her dead.

And because the balm had done its work so quickly, he'd become acutely aware of her long, bare legs, beautiful skin and how much he wanted her.

He glanced down again. He'd stopped toweling, but the turn of his thoughts had brought his cock to full attention. He took it in hand and his breathing grew rough. Thoughts of Emma and her thong filled his head once more. He almost started stroking, but decided he'd better get himself settled down. He had more important things to do than to fire one off.

He wrapped a second towel around his hips, though it took a full minute before the terry cloth lay flat against his body.

He glanced at his blood-stained, sweaty clothes. He'd have to put them back on eventually, but not right now. Maybe later, after the drug Emma had taken wore off. For now, he'd stay in a cleaned up state especially since he was in her home.

The woman had money and beautiful things. Even the carpet had a deep plush feel as he moved back into the bedroom.

Unfortunately for his ever-present desire for the witch, Emma had thrown the comforter off her, then rolled onto her back, legs spread, her arms over her head. Most of her abdomen was exposed.

His gaze followed her curves. She had an unusually narrow waist and he wondered if his hands would fit her all the way around. Once more his gaze fell to the sight of her sex behind a thin violet veil. A narrow strip of auburn hair made his jaw tremble.

He licked his lips and just like that his other problem returned, pushing once more against the towel around his waist.

Tearing his gaze away from her, he moved into a large adjacent dressing room. From the phone conversations, he'd learned that Emma had entered Five Bridges with a trust fund. Her home was large and well-maintained, though he knew for a fact that at least three cartel lieutenants lived in her upscale neighborhood.

But that was life in their world. Gainful employment was hard to come by since the sex and drug trade dominated the economy.

That she'd chosen to serve as a TPS officer without pay was one of the reasons he admired her. She served because she wanted more than anything to help make their world a decent place to live.

He moved toward a large upholstered bench in the center of the room. He was about to sit down, when an unexpected array of clothes hit him hard. The side of the closet he faced held a row of clothing that belonged to a man. A big man. Someone his size.

Emma hadn't said anything to him about having someone in her life, though he'd heard a rumor that she'd once taken up with a shifter. At the time, he'd thought it disgusting. He didn't believe the species should ever mix. However, since their tryst two months ago, he'd been having serious doubts about his beliefs.

But what did it mean she had a man's clothes in her closet? Did they belong to the rumored shifter from Savage Territory?

He sat down on the bench, staring up at the jeans and shirts. There were even a couple pairs of boots below. The man had big feet to match his body, just like Vaughn.

Blood once more pounded in his head, but this time for a different reason. He was jealous as hell.

~ ~ ~

Emma woke up to fingers patting her face. She pushed them away repeatedly, but to no effect. Finally, she was able to open her eyes.

The ghost-girls moved swiftly away from her to hover near the door to her dressing room and seemed to be having a joke at her expense. They were all grinning like crazy. She could tell they were laughing as well, though the sound she heard wasn't the same as the living would have made.

Seeing that she was partially uncovered, she whipped the comforter over her body. She really didn't want Vaughn to see her like this.

She glanced around, but he wasn't in the room. Her bedroom formed the east wing of her home and faced into a large, well-landscaped courtyard. The overall property was a good half-acre and contained over two dozen trees. Because the bed faced into the yard, she could see Vaughn wasn't there, either.

She loved her home. It had been a blessing for the past seven years. She'd been consigned to Five Bridges because an *alter* witch-serum had made its way into a bowl of punch at a party. At least three people had died that night, unable to handle the *alter* process. She'd survived and after a period of adjustment, she'd made it her mission to create an oasis in her new world.

She watched the ghosts fly acrobatically around the room, learning their new skills. After a moment, they lined up once more outside her large walk-in closet. She aimed her telepathy toward the girl in the blue jeans. *Let me guess. Vaughn's in my dressing room?*

The girl nodded and smiled. *He is.*

What's your name?

Becca. Her smile broadened into a grin. *We're glad you're feeling better. My sisters and I think you might need some privacy, though, so we're going to explore Five Bridges. We'll be back in about an hour.*

Wait. Are you saying you have a sense of time as a ghost?

Sure. Her brows rose, then she chuckled. *And we can read clocks, too.* She inclined her head in the direction of Emma's dresser and her antique Tambour.

Well, see ya later. Becca gestured for her sisters to follow and the ghosts suddenly vanished.

Emma threw the comforter back and glanced down at her bare legs and one of her favorite but oh-so-sheer thongs. It was a lovely violet color and showed off her landing strip.

Her cheeks suddenly warmed up. Vaughn had removed her pants, so of course he'd seen her like this. At least she was still wearing her t-shirt and hadn't been completely exposed.

Memories rushed back of the things she'd said to him, about wanting him.

She covered her face with both hands. Oh, God, her spelled medicine had really loosened her tongue.

Well, she couldn't undo what had already been done. She left the bed, then headed to the bathroom. She had dried blood all down her leg and the injury had left an odd smell on her skin. She brushed out her hair, debating whether to wash it as well, but she wasn't sure what the rest of the night would hold. Drying her hair was a long process.

Deciding not to wash it, she wrapped her hair up in a towel, then stepped into the shower. As thoughts of Vaughn filled her head, she took her time soaping up. She was fully healed and alone with him in her house. A shiver raced through her. Would he want to be with her again? Because right now, the only thing she could think about was a repeat of the couch experience.

All a girl could do was ask.

After drying off, she pulled the towel from her head, wrapped her body in another one, then headed to her dressing room.

Once at the threshold, she pushed the door open. She was surprised to find Vaughn sitting on the bench, elbows on knees, head in hands. He wore only a towel wrapped around his waist.

She stayed where she was and watched him for a long moment. He was facing Max's clothes, the shifter she'd loved and lost a few years ago. She hadn't told Vaughn about him yet. She'd been waiting for the right moment, but it had never come. Now he'd seen the clothes. He also had no framework for knowing who they belonged to or why they were still here.

She could feel the weight of Vaughn's emotions as well. She knew he'd lost his sister several years ago. Her name was Beth, the only family Vaughn had, and she'd become a vampire at the same time as Vaughn.

But one night, a large group of lowlife vampires had abducted her right outside Vaughn's home while he watched, then carted her off to another territory. He'd never found her, though he'd spent at least two years trying.

He'd only mentioned it once on the phone, but she'd felt it then as well. The loss of his sister had changed Vaughn, taken him to a dark place from which he'd never fully returned. He'd told Emma repeatedly that he never dated and had no interest in forming a permanent connection to anyone. Five Bridges was a violent place, and he'd been unable to protect his sister. With death always right around the corner, he didn't want to be responsible for another person ever again.

She could relate to his sense of despair and needing to keep his distance.

Shifting her gaze to Max's clothes, tears touched her eyes. Max had barely moved in when he'd been ambushed and killed on his return to Savage Territory. She'd known nothing about it until two nights later when one of Max's friends had called her to let her know. Despair had hit her hard. From that time, she'd sworn off men, sex and dating, just like Vaughn.

Then Vaughn had shown up and the sex they'd shared as well as all these weeks of talking back and forth on the phone had worn down her resistance. She didn't even care that he was a vampire. For that reason alone, she should have shunned him.

Instead, she stood near him in her dressing room and had no plans at all to get dressed, having something else entirely on her mind.

First, though, she needed to tell him about Max. "I see you've found my secret."

He sat up and turned in her direction. "I thought you'd be out for hours." How she loved his deep voice.

She shook her head. "The potion was designed to be quick-acting and fast-leaving." She crossed to Max's clothes, but half-turned toward Vaughn. "You been wondering about these?"

"Yeah, I was." His gray eyes had a pinched look.

"A few years ago, I dated one of the alphas of Savage Territory. I was madly in love with him and thought we'd be together forever. I suppose I should have gotten rid of these a long time ago." She ran her hand over the sleeves of the shirts, one after the other. She'd said good-bye many times and in many different ways. This felt like another farewell coupled with a poignant jolt of grief.

"What happened to him?"

She took hold of the sleeve of the shirt closest to her and couldn't seem to let go. "We'd just moved in together. We'd done the unforgivable as in a shifter, especially an alpha, getting involved with a witch. He was ambushed one night shortly after crossing the main bridge back to Savage. Someone shot him in the back of the head."

"Because of you?"

"I think I made a good excuse."

"And I take it the culprit was never found."

"No." She huffed a sigh. "But I had my suspicions. Max had a powerful challenger in his pack, a real brute by the name of Dagen." She shuddered. "I hated Dagen from the moment I met him. He came onto me every time Max's back was turned."

"Dagen. The name sounds familiar. Right. I met him a couple of times after Beth died. I'd been searching for her and more than once the path of her abduction led to him, but then stopped dead. He had a real stench about him as I recall."

"He has powerful connections to the cartels."

"Figures. So, you think he killed Max?"

"Dagen would never have challenged Max to a straight-up dominance fight because Max would have whipped him in a pit-battle." The shifter territories had sand pits in various parts of Savage to serve as a staging area for a pack challenge.

"You miss him?"

"Everyday. And I'm sorry I never told you about him before now. I just couldn't. I mean, maybe the way he died made it worse. I hated that there was no justice for him. Then Dagen took over the pack. They've all suffered since."

She tilted her head. "The funny thing is, I promised myself I'd never date a shifter again, and I haven't." She smiled ruefully. "But it seems I have trouble being interested in my own *alter* species. Now here you are, a vampire, with a towel around your waist in my dressing room." The air grew electric. "And what I said to you in the bathroom? I'm embarrassed, but it was the truth."

He rose to his feet and drew close. He gently took her arms in his hands. "Em, we almost died out there in the Graveyard. That's what I've been thinking about."

"Uh-huh."

His eyes were low on his lids, and she was pretty sure his towel wasn't fitting him as well as it had been a moment ago.

"We don't have to date, Vaughn. I don't think either of us really wants that. But it's been a lonely stretch since Max died and I want to be with you."

"How long has it been?"

"Five years."

"Shit." His voice had dropped several timbres.

"I'll tell you what went through my head when you launched us into the air. It was the dumbest thing, but I thought I'd be dead soon. And the thought of never getting to have sex with you again really pissed me off. Yet here you are."

"But are you sure you want to do this?"

"Oh, hell, yeah, I'm sure. I've already told you how I feel. I respect you and if this had been a different world I would have shown up quite magically at the restaurants you liked to go to, that sort of thing."

He frowned. "Do women do that?"

"If we didn't, no man would ever find a wife."

His lips actually curved. "You're probably right." He reached down and untucked his towel, letting it fall to the floor.

She drew in a deep slow breath, then took a moment to look him over. He had a gorgeous, heavily muscled body. It was one of the hallmarks of the *alter* species, an increase in strength. Only with Vaughn, it had made him almost godlike.

He had a massive chest with tattoos spanning the breadth. His pecs were full and made her mouth water.

Some witchy part of her, maybe what she'd accessed earlier, came alive as well. She felt her power begin to flow. It was the same energy that could light up the tips of her fingers and send a surge of electricity through his temple and kill him.

But killing wasn't on her mind and all that electricity spread down her neck, over her breasts and rolled toward her sex. When it hit, her whole body writhed.

He reached for her own towel and slowly pulled apart the tucked in section. She felt a sweep of cold air as the terry fell to the floor.

He touched her shoulders, then pulled back. "I'm feeling that electricity of yours again."

"Yes, you'd have to be." The words came out breathy. "Because I'm feeling it, too, all through my body."

Her gaze fell to his cock. He was fully erect and maybe as hungry as she was because she saw moisture beaded at the tip.

He reached for her arms again, only this time he didn't recoil. Instead, he smoothed his hands over her shoulders and down her chest. He ran his hands over her breasts, thumbing each nipple. Her breathing hitched. And she was pretty sure she could see the tips of his fangs.

She moaned. "I love how you're touching me."

He met her gaze, then drew her against him and wrapped her up in his arms. His cock was pressed against her abdomen. He was a big man in every respect and she wanted all that bigness inside her.

He planted his lips on hers and she parted for him so that his tongue slipped inside. He began to drive steadily, making the most exquisite promise of what he planned to do to her.

She arched her hips and slowly moved side to side to feel him better. She suckled his tongue and felt his fangs at the same time.

She'd been with him only once, and he hadn't pierced her throat then. If he did now, she'd fall into an enthralled state from which she couldn't emerge until he wanted her to. This was the main advantage vampires had over witches. She couldn't even use her killing fingers in that condition.

He'd have complete power over her.

Yet somehow, that's exactly what she wanted. "Use your fangs, Vaughn."

He drew back and thumbed her lips. "You sure?"

She nodded. All she knew or even cared about, was that she wanted him drinking from her and she wanted him now. She also knew it didn't have to be at her throat. The thought he'd bite her somewhere else, especially down low, had her sex clenching hard.

"Bury your fangs any place you like."

He moaned heavily. But his face became all twisted up, and he hissed through his teeth.

"What's wrong?"

"Give me a sec. Those words almost made me come."

She chuckled softly and ran her fingers over the short hair above his ears. "Then I'm not alone in how much I need you right now?"

"Do I look like I'm *not* desperate here?" He held his hands wide.

She glanced down at his rigid cock. She drew a little closer and planted her hands on his waist. "I'd love to be on my knees right now, but that wouldn't help much either, would it?"

"No, it wouldn't."

He pushed a long strand of her hair behind her ear. "I've fantasized about being with you again. I've wanted you, every night since I had you on my couch. But I don't see a future here, Em, and it doesn't help that we live in different territories."

She caressed his face. "On opposite sides of a long stretch of barbed wire."

"Yep."

"Then there's the elephant in the room." Would he know what she meant?

"You mean Iris and Connor."

He got it. Connor had been one of his fellow officers in Crescent Territory who fell in love with a witch. Emma knew Iris since she served on the TPS force as well. A month ago, Connor had resigned from the Crescent force and joined the Trib.

Emma wanted Vaughn to know how she felt despite their differences. "Ever since Connor and Iris announced their engagement, it's made it harder than ever to get you out of my mind."

Vaughn nodded. "Same here. But being different *alter* species isn't the only reason. I don't have a lot to give."

She reached up and kissed him. "I know. And I promise you, I don't have high expectations here. In fact, I don't think I have any expectations at all." She then smiled, her lips twisting. "I mean, we're not even sure we'll make it through the night. So how about we focus on what we can do."

She slid her hand from his waist, down his hip and slowly stroked the length of his cock.

His nostrils flared and he groaned once more. "That feels amazing." Yet he caught her hand and made her stop. "Again, way too good." He kissed her on the cheek then her lips.

He drew her close once more and as she parted for him, his tongue moved inside. She gripped his arms and fondled his muscles, one of her fantasies come to life. She slipped into telepathy. *I've wanted to touch you again, Vaughn. I love the feel of you under my hands.* She dug her nails in a little and again he groaned, arching his hips at the same time.

Her turn to moan.

She drew back. "I loved our time on your couch. I know it was really fast, but it was so good. I never felt free enough during any of our phone calls to tell you that, but it was one of the best experiences of my life."

He nodded. "For me, too. But I don't want what happens right now to be fast. And there's something I want to do for you, something I've been thinking about for weeks."

Her sex grew needy with the various ideas that flew through her mind. She knew what kind of lover he would be. The sex two months ago may have been quick, but he made sure she was satisfied. She could still hear his words. *Are you with me baby? You ready? I want you to come.*

Even thinking about it made her hot all over. "So what is it you want to do?"

He released her, then took her hand and led her to the bench. "Ever since I saw your sex behind that sheer purple fabric, I've been hungry."

Her breaths grew shallow. "How hungry?"

His smile was wicked. "I want you on your back, but put your hips right here at the edge of the bench."

Emma sat down, then stretched out. Vaughn slowly pushed her legs apart and knelt between them, sliding his arms under her thighs.

As he kissed her abdomen, her pelvis rolled. She could hardly breathe when he moved his lips lower and lower, kissing her each time then letting her feel his tongue on her skin.

When he reached her mound, he kissed her sex over and over, yet more like worshiping than getting down to business. She loved it. Loved that though he was as anxious as she was to really engage, this lovely piece of oral pleasure rocked her world.

When he tilted slightly and she felt him drag the side of his fang over her folds, she gasped. What was he going to do?

Desire pulled inside her, a long grip on what she wished was there. "Are you going to bite me?"

"Just a shallow nip right here." His tongue hit one of her most tender spots. "Then I'll be sucking."

She didn't hesitate. "Do it."

He blew between her folds, which had her gasping all over again.

The sting of his fangs came next, in two different spots so that she cried out.

He only licked at the wounds first, catching what she could feel had started to flow from her skin. Something in his vampire saliva kept the wounds from closing up, though later he could release a different chemical to seal the cuts. But not until he was ready.

Each lick was a firm glide over her sex. Her hips rocked heavily now. She was already close to orgasm and they'd barely gotten started.

His voice entered her mind. *Can you talk like this?*

Yes. Even her telepathic voice sounded breathless.

Good, because I don't want to stop what I'm doing. But I want you to know that your blood tastes like a flower, like something exotic. My God, Emma.

I love what you're doing to me, Vaughn. I love that you've bitten me and that I'm feeding you. I'm also feeling very strange, almost dizzy, because of the thrall. Yet it feels fantastic.

It's supposed to keep you in a state of complete submission.

She loved the sensation. *It's amazing, like feeling heat all the way to my bones. I couldn't move away from you if I wanted to. No wonder some witches I know seek out vampires just for this kind of pleasure.*

If you like this, you're going to love what I do next.

What did he mean? She held her breath, waiting.

That's when he took her in his mouth and began to suck in earnest. He drank from the wounds, and at the same time, continued to drive her toward ecstasy. A cry left her throat. He sucked harder, tugging at all her sensitive folds and at the same time feeding from what kept flowing.

The dizzying thrall seemed to intensify and suddenly the orgasm arrived, rolling over her in heavy, erotic waves. She gripped his shoulders, pushing her sex against his mouth and savoring each tug on her flesh.

He stayed with her until the last bit of pleasure faded then drifted away. She lay lax on the bench, her arms hanging down on either side.

He swiped the wounds with his tongue to seal them, then lifted up to look at her. "I could spend hours right here, making you come repeatedly."

She nodded. "I'd love it, too." She became aware that the sealing of the wounds had ended the thrall. She was no longer dizzy, yet she already missed the sensation of being caught by him.

She looked into his intense, gray eyes dilated with need. Affection for him warmed her chest. Sex had always meant more to her than just the physical and because of all the phone calls, she knew Vaughn now, knew him well.

A feeling very much like love expanded in her chest. But at almost the same moment, she repressed the feeling. This was Five Bridges, a hellish place that had already cost her so much. Did she really want to go down that road again?

He rose up slightly and kissed her abdomen several times. "You're looking very serious, Em."

"This is so strange but wonderful to be with you right now. I'm loving this stolen time of ours." She ran her fingers down his cheek. "And being enthralled was amazing, especially knowing you could have killed me if you'd wanted to. Very dangerous and erotic."

For some reason this made him smile.

"Are you laughing at me?"

"Not exactly. I was picturing how long it would take to deplete your blood supply from where I was feeding." His lips curved.

She couldn't help but laugh. "How very wicked, but what a way to go."

He chuckled again and once more she caressed his face. "I love that we're doing this, but I never thought it would happen."

"Me, neither."

~ ~ ~

Vaughn stared into Emma's passion-drenched eyes. The taste of her blood and her sex combined was still in his mouth and kept him hard as a rock. But what surprised him was how much her blood had powered him up. His muscles felt pumped, and for a moment, he could feel what it was for Emma to be a witch.

He didn't know how much time they actually had together, but he intended to make the most of it.

He stood up and looked Emma over head-to-foot. Her breasts were full, her nipples peaked from the orgasm. As he leaned over her, he planted one hand near her shoulder to support his weight. He ran his free hand from one pelvic bone to the next then over the soft indentation of her lower abdomen. He moved his hand upward, traveling over her navel then farther to caress each breast.

"You're beautiful, Em. Every bit of you."

Her hands moved over his shoulders and arms at the same time, a sensual fondling of his muscles. He could tell she liked his body by the way she plucked at each bulge. He flexed when she dug her nails in.

He leaned close and took his time suckling each of her breasts. When her moans grew urgent, he knew it was time to move things along. "Put your hands on my shoulders."

She obeyed readily.

"Now hold on. I'm going to shift your position." He gripped her waist and smiled because his fingers fit all the way around her. With a smooth motion, he lifted her to lie more fully on the bench.

She held her arms out to him and he eased down between her legs. The bench had a nice width but he was a big man so there still wasn't a lot of room. She made it work by surrounding his hips with her legs.

"I've been wanting to be this close to you again, more than you can know."

"Me, too." She ran her fingers through the close crop of hair on the sides of his head. "This is so sexy, Vaughn. I love these tattoos. And I've imagined doing this, touching you here, wondering whether your hair was wiry or silky." She smiled. "It's kind of both."

He kissed her then, rimming her lips with his tongue. *I love your body, your mouth, your sex. And that you've thought about me.*

As he continued to kiss her, she slid a hand low and slowly stroked his cock. *I've had dozens of fantasies about doing this with you, touching you, savoring the feel of your muscular body. But this is so much better.*

I love how you're stroking me, Em. But I need to be inside you. Are you ready for me?

She moaned softly. "God, yes."

He shifted just enough to take his cock in hand and drew back to look down at her. He wanted to watch as he entered her body. When he pressed his cock against her opening, her whole body undulated and she moaned at the same time. She was streaming for him as well, which made his entrance an easy glide.

He took his time, savoring every sensation, the way her hips rolled with each thrust. She caressed his shoulders, then his arms, making her way down his back, to his waist, until she pressed her nails into his ass.

He thrust steadily. "I'm feeling your witchness, Em, that soft electric feeling you give off, only this time it's inside you and it feels great."

She closed her eyes and he felt her gather more of her power. "I can feel it, too." She opened her eyes and met his gaze. A cry left her throat. "And I'm about ready to explode."

The time had come. He increased his speed, pumping steadily, working her up. He watched as pleasure flowed over her features, a lift of her brows, an arch of her neck, the way she almost grimaced when she took a breath.

Once more, he felt her open herself to her power and small jolts of electricity had him on the brink.

"Faster," she whispered. "I'm going to come."

"I won't be far behind."

He drove into her hard now, a quick, strong rhythm. She writhed beneath him. Then her neck arched and she was crying out.

The sight of her ecstasy tightened his balls, and he began to release. At the same time, her power kept the soft electrical shocks going that intensified his orgasm. His voice opened wide and he shouted, joining her cries.

Pleasure rolled, peaked and rolled some more.

And just when he was dialing down, he felt an odd sensation in his groin. "Holy shit, I don't believe this."

He began to drive into her once more, his cock as hard as before.

She met his gaze. "That feels so good. Again, Vaughn?" Her brows rose. She gripped his biceps and moaned.

"Your witchness and your blood has done something to me. So, yeah. Hell, yeah, we're going again."

He held her gaze, moving faster than before, thrusting and loving every second of it. "Come for me, baby."

Her lips parted. "Yes. Now. Oh, God."

The orgasm barreled down on him, and he roared once more, a sound that caught her passionate cries and carried them in waves around the dressing room.

When at last the moment of ecstasy dimmed, he began to come back to himself.

He looked down at Emma and saw that tears spilled from her eyes. He froze in place. "Did I hurt you?"

"No. Oh, God, no, it was just so unbelievable. Truly, Vaughn, it was more than perfect."

Relief flooded him. "For a minute there—"

"You didn't hurt me. I'm just overcome. I swear you took me to the center of the universe and back. Though now I'm convinced you just spoiled me the rest of my life for any other man."

He looked down at her, seeing her as if for the first time. She was his kind of woman. He would have been drawn to her outside of Five Bridges before his *alter.*

But he couldn't pretend their world didn't exist. He'd become a creature he despised, not-human-anymore, and she was a witch.

He pulled out of her, a sense of loss piercing him so hard, he couldn't look at Emma any longer. Visions of his sister's abduction filled his head, only this time, he saw Emma being taken from him.

He couldn't do this, not with her, not with anyone.

"Vaughn, wait." She grabbed at his arm as he moved away, but he didn't want her to see him like this.

He wasn't even sure what he was feeling, but it felt like death all over again.

~ ~ ~

Emma cupped herself between her thighs. Sex was always messy without a condom.

She saw the discarded towels. Half rolling off the bench, she grabbed one and jammed it against her sex.

She lowered herself to sit on the carpet of the dressing room for a couple of minutes, trying to collect herself. She knew why Vaughn had left her so abruptly. She was feeling it as well, how close the sex had brought them. It almost felt as though they'd bonded in some mysterious way.

But she knew his suffering, that he hated being an *alter* vampire almost as much as she despised being a witch. She also suspected that thoughts of Beth had overtaken him. Vaughn considered her abduction the greatest failure of his life. He was a proud man. Not being able to protect his sister had crushed him.

And there wasn't anything she could do. Beth had been taken to Elegance Territory and had probably been used up in one of the sex clubs, her body buried afterward in the desert somewhere.

When Vaughn had said he had nothing to give, he'd meant it.

The truth was, as much as she felt for Vaughn, how tender her heart had become toward him, she didn't want a commitment either. Max's death had ruined something inside her as well, and she doubted she'd ever feel differently.

When she heard the shower running, she rose to her feet, left the dressing room and headed across her bedroom to the bathroom. Reaching the threshold, she was going to tell him not to worry, that she had no expectations. But that's when she saw him, palms flat on the tile wall of the shower stall, his head bent beneath the stream of water, shoulders slumped.

Tears started to her eyes.

She didn't ask permission to join him. She simply padded her way across the bathroom floor, tossed her towel on the floor near the laundry hamper, then entered the shower.

She moved in behind him and slid her arms around his waist. She held him as tight as she could.

"Don't." But his voice broke.

"Fuck that, Vaughn. We're here right now and it's enough."

"It's not enough. Emma, how could I have found you now, in this hellhole we've come to, when we've got a goddam madman after us?"

He turned, breaking her hold on his waist. But she threw herself against his chest and his arms surrounded her in a strong embrace. She wept. She hadn't expected Vaughn to care, not really. Or to feel anything that matched her own heart. *I feel the same way. I just found you. And now—*

And now—

After a moment, she lifted her face to his. "Vaughn, you don't need to say anything else, and I'm pretty wrecked still about what happened to the girls. So how about we shift gears a little. I mean, I don't expect to live out this night or if I do, to make it through the next few days. Loghry has an army and we're just two people."

He nodded, smoothing her hair with his hand. "He'll hunt for us and probably take us both out."

"Then before he does, I'd be happy to locate a couple of automatic rifles and knock on his mansion door. What do you say?"

He thumbed her cheek and leaned down to kiss her. "I was thinking the same thing."

CHAPTER THREE

The shifter's clothes were a near fit for Vaughn. Max had been a big man as many of the werewolves were, especially the alphas.

In any other circumstance, Vaughn wouldn't have put on another man's clothes. But he was stuck in Emma's house, and for her sake the last thing he wanted was to wear his blood-stained leathers and tank top.

She had a beautiful home with a dozen rooms and extensive, well-kept landscaping. He stood outside in the backyard, impressed by the grouping of shrubs and beds full of flowers. A large number of full-grown trees rounded out a solid look and would provide a lot of cooling shade during the summer months.

Halfway down the yard, he could see an owl, with a unique white face, perched in the most central tree. Vaughn was pretty sure it was called a barn owl, a creature Emma no doubt used as a familiar.

A gray-striped cat paced near the same tree. The pair of critters represented an essential element for an *alter* witch. Vaughn didn't get it, but cats and owls served witches, adding to their power.

They both stared at him as though having human thoughts. Each appeared to be taking his measure.

"Hey."

He turned at the sound of Emma's voice and watched her cross the threshold to the backyard. She wore a light green t-shirt and her usual jeans, a great look for her. She'd arranged the front part of her long hair in a top knot again. She was a beautiful woman with creamy white skin, rich auburn hair and emerald green eyes.

She moved toward him. "Have you met Toby and Stormy?"

He couldn't help but be a little amused. "Those names are too precious, Em."

She chuckled. "I know, I know. But that's what came to me when I invoked one of my first spells. You can make fun of me if you want. Sometimes, I'm plain-old embarrassed."

"So which one is Toby?"

She inclined her head toward the tree. "My cat. I've had him with me almost as long as I've been here. He showed up on my doorstep as a lost kitten. Now he helps guard my property." The cat, hearing his name, headed in Emma's direction.

He could tell she was teasing about the last bit because of the quirk to her lips. Though he'd only been with her twice now, he realized she often smiled with a charming twist of her lips.

He held out his arm to her and she joined him, sliding her own arm around his waist. When he pulled her close, she leaned her head into the well of his shoulder.

So much affection flowed through his chest that he had the worst impulse to tell her he loved her.

After he'd been with her in the dressing room, he'd become overwhelmed with a profound sense of loss. He had nothing to give Emma, and they had a death sentence.

For reasons he couldn't explain, thoughts of how he'd lost his sister had gained a foothold. He'd basically run from those feelings only to find Emma pressed up against him in the shower. He'd shed some tears, which still pissed him off. He didn't want to get caught up in something like this, and it sucked that for the first time in his entire eleven years in Five Bridges, he was close to falling in love.

There. He'd admitted the whole damn thing to himself. Hell, he'd probably tumbled hard the moment he found her pulling boxes of flowers out of Loghry's van that night.

Easton had sent him to Sentinel Bridge, which separated Elegance Territory from the human part of Phoenix. His boss had wanted Vaughn to bring a delivery van safely through as a personal favor to him.

When he asked Emma what she was doing, she'd told him straight out that she was saving some girls. He'd cursed Easton under his breath, then pitched in and helped.

He could still remember her flushed cheeks and the glitter in her green eyes. Together, they'd unloaded the rest of the flowers then lifted the lid of the hidden container. The sight of the triplets, drugged, unconscious, and jammed into such a small space, still burned in his mind.

After he and Emma had driven them home personally, crossing the U.S. government controlled border to get them back to their families in Phoenix, he'd been pumped. She had as well. That's when they'd celebrated first with a few beers, then sex on his sofa.

Now they were here, knowing full well Loghry wouldn't rest until they were both dead.

He squeezed her shoulders gently. "So, I've been thinking. I can't risk going home, not now. But I have several fellow officers I trust, and I can get some weapons sent to a Crescent Territory drop point, maybe a couple of AR-15s and some ammo."

"Sounds good." Emma released him, then started to pace a few feet away. Toby had drawn close, though he sat and eyed her movements, his tail twitching. "But I think I should spend some time with my brew pot. I just have this feeling ... "

"About what?"

She stopped and met his gaze. "Earlier, when I was in the ditch and opened myself up to my power, I had a moment of seeing the future in a series of images, like snapshots. At the time, I set it aside, because I felt the need to focus on the girls, to help their spirits move out of their bodies. But right now, I want to see if I can tap into the future. It might help us."

"You believe that?" He was unfamiliar with witch things in the same way she no doubt couldn't relate to his blood-cravings. Hell, it had taken him a couple of years to accept his physical need to pierce the vein.

For a moment, his mind got caught on exactly how he'd tapped into her blood while in her dressing room. His nostrils flared. He wanted to do it again, maybe tap into a different place next time. His gaze fell to her breasts, though he glanced away quickly.

She shrugged. "I at least want to see if I can engage with some form of prescience. I can't promise anything, but I've always known I had a lot of latent ability."

He made a point to keep his gaze on her face. "I've always valued that about you, Emma. Before I got to know you, I thought most witches were power hungry—" He almost added 'monsters', which wouldn't have helped their situation.

Her lips quirked. "Most who work hard at expanding their witch abilities are after more power, so I understand your disdain. For me, it was different, but not necessarily better, as time has proved. I've been pretending I'm still human. And I'm not.

"But what ticks me off is that right now, if I was a stronger witch, we'd have a much better chance of taking Loghry down. Instead, it's sort of like fighting a forest fire with a bucket of water. But I'm done with that and maybe you should prepare yourself, because I might become what you despise the most."

He could sense her distress. He took hold of her arms in a gentle grip. "Hey, I could never think badly of you. I know your character, and I trust you. I do."

"But what if I'm all spelled up and become the kind of witch who no longer cares, who could actually hurt you?"

"Then we'll deal with it. Right now, I don't give a damn if you grow hooves and horns so long as it will help us battle Loghry."

She grinned. "Oh, now there's a lovely picture."

She turned and headed back into the house. "I'll be in my spellroom. And, by the way, Stormy and Toby approve of you, in case you hadn't noticed. Stormy, the owl, would have turned his back on you if he hadn't thought you were amazing."

Vaughn glanced at the owl first, who still stared at him, then looked down at the cat. Toby was doing a figure-eight around his ankles, weaving in and out and purring. He'd never been much of a cat person, but he'd felt the same way about witches until Emma.

There was always a first time.

From inside the house, Emma gestured to the west wing. "My spellroom is this way, if you need me."

When she disappeared down the hall, he called Robert Brannick, one of his good friends and a fellow officer at Crescent Border Patrol. He reached the station and got routed to Lily in dispatch.

She kept her voice low. "Easton's been asking about you, wanting to know the second you call in. We all heard what happened at the Graveyard. Are you okay?"

"I'm fine."

"You're not shot up and bleeding to death?"

"Nope."

"How about that TPS officer you were with? The witch. Did she survive?"

"GSW to the right calf, but she's all healed up. She'd made some kind of healing potion. It worked fast."

Lily whistled softly. "That's some kind of power."

He'd known Emma had potential, but even he'd been surprised when he'd felt her power at the Graveyard and of course later, when he'd made love to her.

Again, his mind got caught on his drive to get her on her back again. He'd thought making love to her would settle him down. The opposite appeared to be true.

Lily's voice broke his train of thought. "Vaughn, what the hell is going on? At least a dozen of your brothers-in-arms were ready to take on the entire Elegance Border Patrol for what they did. Easton had five of our own jailed to keep them from going apeshit because of the attack."

"Was Brannick one of them? Is he locked up?"

"No, thank God. But you know what a cool head he has. Though, I'm not sure I've ever seen him look as grim as he did when he heard what happened."

Vaughn wasn't surprised that some of his fellow officers had taken the attack hard. It was one thing for vampires to be killed by dark coven witches and warlocks as part of executions or even sacrifices. But an assassination attempt by a police force was a different animal altogether.

"I won't pretend I'm not in trouble. Loghry is behind this attack."

"Seriously? The wizard who owns all those sex clubs in Elegance? Oh-h-h-h, wait a minute. It's retribution for the girls you and that witch rescued, isn't it?"

"Yes. He abducted the triplets again, then tortured and killed them. So, yeah, this was personal."

Lily got very quiet, then finally asked in a voice full of despair. "Are we going to see you again?"

She'd asked the question of the night. "Hell if I know. But I'm not going down without a fight, which is why I need to talk to Brannick. I need his help, and I need you to keep this on the down low. Can you do that or will this get you in trouble with Easton?"

Silence followed for a few difficult seconds. When Lily spoke, he heard granite in her voice. "I'll do whatever needs to be done. Easton is a pig. Just tell me what you need me to do. I'll come to you, if that will help. I'll walk out of this building right now and to hell with the calls that come in. There are only a handful of you men on the right side of things and Vaughn, I tell you this with all sincerity, I'd lay down my life for you. So, I mean it when I say *ask anything of me*."

His throat grew tight, and he had to take a minute before he could answer her. He swallowed hard a couple of times. "Tell you what. Go ahead and contact Brannick directly. Tell him I need weapons, a couple of AR-15s and ammo for my Glock. Have him take a duffel to the safe house in central Crescent. He'll know the one I mean. I'm not sure when I can get there to retrieve it, but I'll call you back in a few to check on timing."

"You got it. Shit, Easton just walked in."

He heard the clicking sound of the disconnect and didn't attempt to call back. Lily knew what she had to do, both to contact Brannick and to keep herself safe as well as to deal with Easton.

The chief of Crescent Border Patrol was in deep with the cartels that supported Loghry. Any suspect move on Lily's part could get her killed.

But how the hell were he and Emma supposed to bust into Loghry's mansion when security was known to be the best in Five Bridges?

~ ~ ~

Emma loved her spellroom. It overlooked her garden at the northwest side of her property, and whenever she was in the space, her owl would fly to the very old Indian laurel that shaded her French doors. She often threw them wide when she was mixing a brew in her cauldron, which she did now. She called to Stormy and he fluffed his wings in response.

When she'd first become an *alter* witch, she'd felt compelled to create what for every witch or warlock was a very private, personal space. She'd visited a number of spellrooms and from her response to each, she designed the best layout for her own spellcasting and brewmaking equipment.

She hadn't been so opposed to exploring her craft in the early days. It was only a few weeks later that she'd made the decision to permanently limit her spellcasting powers. She'd learned to her horror that many powerful witches belonged to dark covens that routinely slaughtered other species, especially vampires.

On the west wall of her room was a hutch she'd had fitted out with several shelves. Glass canisters, each bearing black labels and gold calligraphy, contained dozens of dried herbs, seeds and pods, as well as mushrooms, leaves, roots, and flowers. Her housekeeper kept the room immaculate, but from the time Emma had filled each container, she hadn't used but a handful of the contents in seven years. A spell kept them all from deteriorating.

She lit the gas flame beneath her cauldron and added a cup of purified water and a bay leaf. She had one goal, to see as much of the future as she could so that she and Vaughn could plan accordingly. Bay always increased a sense that the future was only a thought away.

Once the water was releasing steam, she moved to stand in front of her canisters. She repeated the words of a spell meant to invoke prescience. As she touched each canister, she pulled the ones forward that spoke to her.

She lined up the canisters and from each withdrew the amount that called to her. One by one, she ground them up in her marble mortar using a matching pestle, then added them to her cast iron, brew pot.

As soon as the recipe was complete, Toby hurried into her spellroom and rubbed around her ankles. The presence of her cat told her she was on the right path.

With the water boiling and the fragrant steam rising, she felt the room grow even more focused, more centered.

She bent over the cauldron and closed her eyes. Using both hands, she wafted the steam toward her and let the essence of the brew flow through her nostrils and into her lungs. A faint dizziness assailed her mind.

She repeated the process several times.

When the entire room was filled with magic, she turned the flame off. She set a glass measuring cup on the small filling platform, and with a pair of oven mitts and taking great care, she tipped the cauldron to release the brew.

When the measuring cup held the liquid, she filled her sink with an inch of tepid water and settled the cup in the basin to cool the boiled liquid.

While she waited for the potion to become drinkable, she gathered bay infused candles and arranged seven of them in an arc at the head of her purple velvet *chaise-longue.*

She changed out the tepid water, adding back a much cooler temperature. She did this several times very gradually until the brew was drinkable.

Pouring the potion into a red ceramic cup, she held it with both hands then moved to the French doors.

She called to her owl. "Stormy, come in please. I need you with me." She stepped aside to make room for him through the doorway.

The owl dipped off the branch and once clear of the leaves flapped his broad wings a few times then glided through the open doors to a perch in the center of the room. Stormy created a layer of protection for Emma as she slowly imbibed the potion designed to enhance her ability to see the future.

When the red cup was empty, she slid it beneath the *chaise-longue.*

She stretched out and allowed the brew to work within her mind. After a few minutes, she set about casting her spell, invoking words she'd written years ago, calling the future to her.

She waited.

But nothing happened.

She could feel the spell all around her and inside her. But the power she'd experienced in the Graveyard seemed to hover at a significant distance.

Spreading out her arms, she once more opened herself up to her power.

But again, it was as though she was stunted in some way she didn't yet understand.

She sat up and instinctively knew everything should have worked. She glanced at Toby who eyed her with what she thought was a rather skeptical expression.

She shifted her gaze to Stormy. "What do you have to say?" The owl rose up once and flapped his wings, then twisted midair to face away from her toward the door leading into the hallway.

When Toby trotted toward the door as well, she knew her familiars were trying to tell her something.

She rose to her feet and followed in Toby's wake.

He went straight to Vaughn, who now sat in the front living room, ensconced in the large, dark leather chair she'd bought for Max when he'd first moved in. He held his phone in one hand, checking emails, a heavy frown on his brow.

For some reason, images of making love with him in the dressing room flowed through her mind. Her entire body tingled at the memory and her eyes burned with sudden affection.

He looked great in Max's t-shirt and jeans. He was also barefoot, which made her smile. Even sitting down, he looked like a warrior, shoulders broad and the snug dark gray t-shirt conformed to thick pecs. He had strong cheekbones that angled to an equally strong jawline. His nose had a slightly hawkish appearance.

He looked up at her. "Hey."

His steely gray eyes melted her. For a moment, she couldn't remember why she'd even come in here. At least, not until Toby jumped up on the arm of the chair. Vaughn's hand went to the cat's back, and he pet him absently all the way down to his tail.

Vaughn's eyes narrowed. "Everything okay?"

On some level, she knew she was behaving oddly since she hadn't said a word. But it might have been the spell keeping her off-balance.

She could feel the brew working in her now as it hadn't in the spellroom. Images began moving through her mind like a carousel, spinning round and round, similar to her experience in the Graveyard. Though she knew the future was right there, she couldn't access the snapshots.

She took a step toward Vaughn, then another. The carousel began to slow and a couple of the images, this time of a pine forest, appeared very clearly. But nothing more.

"Emma?"

She lifted a finger. "Give me a sec."

She took a few more steps in Vaughn's direction and the spell tightened. More images fell into place. "I think I need you," she said.

A soft smile touched his lips. "You do?"

She didn't mistake the look of pure affection on his face. She realized her words had a second meaning. But rather than respond, she pondered the question.

Did she need him?

God, yes. To talk to her on the phone, to ease her, to sex her up, to make her time in Five Bridges bearable, and to help her feel safe when she was nothing but vulnerable because an evil wizard wanted her dead.

After a moment, she returned his smile. "I wish things were different. So much."

He nodded slowly. "Me, too. But I'm guessing you have something on your mind other than our relationship."

Back to reality.

"I'm sensing you're needed in my spellroom. I know it doesn't make sense, at least it doesn't to me, but I think you might be able to help me access the future."

He was on his feet and moving in her direction before she'd finished her thought. Her throat grew tight all over again. She'd spoken a handful of words about what she needed and he was right there for her, ready to help.

How was she *not* supposed to fall in love with him?

Her heart warmed all over again as he drew close. She liked so much about Vaughn already, but his willingness to support her witchness meant a great deal. She knew how much he hated and feared her kind. The dark covens routinely trapped vampires with their spells, then killed them.

Yet here was Vaughn, trusting her and supporting her.

The moment he drew within three feet of her, the carousel moving within her mind stopped and the future was right there. She felt dizzy and would have fallen, but he caught her arms with his hands and held her upright.

"What's wrong?"

How could she explain? "Nothing. When you touched me, I finally had access to the future. I just don't know why you're having this kind of effect on me."

"Are you saying you couldn't do it on your own?"

"That's right. Earlier, when I put all the ingredients into a potion for getting a look into the future, very little happened, not even when I opened myself up to my witch power. But when I came out here, the power increased incrementally each time I got closer to you. In fact, both Stormy and Toby encouraged me in your direction. For whatever reason, Vaughn, you're connected to my abilities. Will you join me in my spellroom?"

He'd never looked more serious. "Of course. Whatever you need."

~ ~ ~

Every vampire part of Vaughn resisted Emma's request. Power vibrated in the air around her with more of those small bursts of electricity, though she didn't seem to notice. And the closer he drew to her spellroom, the stronger the instinct rose to get away from her witchness.

When he reached the threshold, his feet refused to budge. He even looked down at them.

Emma turned back in his direction, her gaze sliding to his feet as well. "What's wrong? Why are you still standing in the hall?"

"I'm a vampire, remember? My instincts tell me I'm walking into hell."

She opened her mouth to speak, then closed it. She took a deep breath. "Remember when you bit me?"

Why was she asking that? "Yes. Of course."

"You held me in thrall. You could have killed me. But I trusted you. Right now, I need you to trust me that I would never hurt you."

He shook his head, fists on hips. "This isn't personal, Em."

His gaze fell to her hands, to the tips of her index and middle fingers. One touch to the temple of his forehead or to the base of his neck, a single jolt of power, and he'd be dead.

When he didn't move, she drew close and planted her hands on his arms. "I need you in here. I can't do this without you, and believe me, if there was any other way, I'd do it."

Her touch sang with energy, but instead of recoiling, a strong sensation filled his chest. It felt strangely like a bond he already had with her, though amplified when her witchy power began to rise. After a moment, he realized something else was in play as well. He was experiencing not just Emma's witch energy but her determination to do some good. The shift in focus away from her killing potential to what drove her right now, shoved his instincts into the background.

"Vaughn, all I care about is taking Loghry down."

His lips curved. "I love that about you." Without thinking, he moved inside her spellroom, then responded to a different kind of instinct and took her in his arms.

He kissed her hard, letting her know how much he respected her. She uttered a small cry as she wrapped her arms around his neck. He could feel she was on her tip-toes. She wasn't short for a woman, probably five-ten, but he was damn tall at six-six.

When her lips parted, he deepened the kiss, thrusting his tongue inside. She responded with a moan and pressed her body up against his. She glided her hips back and forth in an effort to feel his arousal. He helped her out by moving one of his hands, grabbing her bottom and pressing her up against him.

He drew back just enough to meet her gaze. "Is that what you want?"

She nodded with a series of quick, hungry jerks of her head. "Vaughn, this is crazy, the way I feel about you. And if we had time—"

"I know. But I'll make you a promise that if we survive the night, I'll take you to bed and I will be thorough."

He watched her eyelids fall to half-mast. "Will you bite me again?"

Once more his lips curved. "Anywhere you want me to." He lifted a hand and caressed her breast, thumbing her peaked nipple. "It can be very erotic right here." He ran his thumb in a circle.

She gasped. "I never thought I'd want a vampire to do these kinds of things to me."

She closed her eyes. He could tell she was making a real effort to compose herself. She chuckled softly as her lids flipped open. "Wish we would have met in the real world."

He thumbed her cheek and offered another kiss, though this one was gentle. "I've thought the same thing."

She pulled away from him completely, but took his hand. "I'm not sure how this should work except that I need to recline and focus." She led him across the room.

Stormy sat on his perch, watching him. On the left, was a cabinet with a lot of glass canisters and beyond that a work area with a cauldron, very witchy.

On the right, was her *chaise-longue* with lit candles arranged at the top. Despite all the evidence of her *alter* species, his instincts remained very distant, and in their place was an odd kind of acceptance.

He watched as Emma reclined, then waved him forward. He joined her, standing over her like a sentinel and maybe that was the point. Maybe he needed to guard her while she summoned powers she'd admitted avoiding most of her witch life.

Toby once more flowed around his ankles, purring and rubbing his whiskered cheeks against his jeans. He didn't know how, but he could feel the cat's approval of him. Again, he smiled. The whole thing was way beyond anything he thought he'd ever experience as a vampire.

As he stared down at Emma, at her long, auburn hair spilled over the purple velvet, he knew that if they both somehow miraculously survived, he'd never want to let her go.

~ ~ ~

Emma had meant to sink into her witchy spell right away, but she felt something surprising from Vaughn. She opened her eyes and looked up at him. His brows were pinched tight together. He didn't look concerned exactly, more like aware. "Everything okay?"

"It is. You do whatever you need to do and tell me where you want me."

"You're perfect right where you are."

"I can kneel."

"Not necessary, at least I don't think so."

This time when she closed her eyes, she let her arms relax beside her body and forced her feet and legs to lose their usual ready-for-action tension. She turned her hands palms up and summoned her power again.

What came this time felt like a whirlwind. Her back arched off the *chaise-longue* and she heard Vaughn call out her name.

She opened her eyes and saw the triplets had returned and were flying rapidly around the room, but they weren't laughing this time.

Something else was going on.

She panted through the waves of energy that kept hitting her, then forced herself to focus on the seat of her power, deep within her body. The carousel of images had returned but flew way too fast.

She suddenly felt Vaughn's hand gripping hers.

She didn't open her eyes this time, but an amazing thing happened because of Vaughn's touch. The images slowed and began to move in a steady progression through her head, more like a movie now than a series of snapshots. She also kept Loghry in the forefront of her mind and pictured his mansion in Elegance.

She was sure she'd soon see either the wizard or his home. Instead, the images showed the inside doors of a large delivery truck, the kind that could carry furniture or large crates.

She didn't understand why she was looking at a truck until the images slowly pivoted so that she faced the interior. Her heart constricted. She could see five teen girls huddled together, with a sixth unconscious on the floor. Each bump in the road sent more than one of them slamming against the hard metal sides of the truck. Groans of pain followed.

So where was this?

The worst roads in Five Bridges were in the Graveyard and in Savage Territory, the latter being several square miles allotted to the *alter* wolf portion of the province. Wolves preferred a forested space to run when they shifted, so a lot of Savage had been planted with trees while the roads had been broken up and sent to a dump site.

The images suddenly withdrew from the interior so that she could see the lettering on the side: Willow Creek Office Furniture. She floated along with the truck, but felt the presence of the triplets as she moved.

The vision took her higher into the air. She was definitely in Savage Territory since the truck entered one of several pine forests planted by *alter* shifters years ago. Wolves preferred forests. It took a lot of water initially, but the city built a reclamation plant just to serve the acres of pine. Better to keep wolves happy than have them busting out of Five Bridges and terrorizing the Phoenix population.

The roads were rough and the original cement and asphalt city blocks long gone. The truck bounced like it did, because it traveled over a lot of dirt.

But what did this truckload of teenage girls have to do with Loghry?

The truck finally began to slow as it drew near a small strip center, though the area was still completely surrounded by pine forest. The driver got out and looked at his watch. "We made it just before midnight.

We get a bonus." He was a tall, lean warlock who did a happy dance in the middle of the uneven dirt road.

Rage rolled through Emma at his antics. The bastard was delivering human females destined for the Savage sex trade and he was smiling because he'd be paid extra for being early.

His partner, another warlock, called to him. "Get moving. You know I don't trust these damn shifters to deliver on their promises. They'd as soon kill us as pay us."

"You ain't shitting on my good mood. I'll have money to spend in the clubs tonight. You ever been with a shifter female? They're real animals in bed." He laughed at his joke.

The images took Emma over the top of the truck. The men went inside a rundown building that used to be a real estate company. Half the lettering on the glass window was faded. Pine needles covered most of the landscape in a reddish brown haze.

The warlocks returned a moment later. A shifter came out with them, a burly man chewing on a cigar and wearing a stained, white tank top. He moved to the truck, opened the doors and peered inside, then immediately afterward slammed the door shut.

"Next time, use the damn delivery entrance, morons."

The warlocks hopped back in and drove the truck around the corner.

Once more, the image sent Emma into the air and over the building. The rear area was a short alley with what looked like storage rental units behind. The truck maneuvered and began backing through the gates.

Her heart rate rose as she saw the sign inside the yard: Daniel D. Loghry, Proprietor. No Trespassing. All Violators Will Be Prosecuted.

Suddenly, the images scrambled like her neurons started misfiring. Pain rushed through her head, and she sat up screaming.

Vaughn dropped to his knees beside the *chaise-longue*, then wrapped her up in his arms. She clung to him, shaking.

"You're okay. You're okay." He repeated the words over and over until she began to calm down.

The ghosts hovered nearby, barely moving at all. She had a sense they'd been affected as well.

"I feel like something evil pressed on me and disrupted what I was seeing."

She rested her head on his shoulder until the trembling passed and the pain was gone. Even then, she stayed put because it felt so good to feel his hands rubbing up and down her back.

She slipped into telepathy. *Thank you. I don't know what happened. I could see all the images as clear as anything. Then suddenly, it felt like I had an electric eggbeater inside my head.*

She felt him chuckle. *I don't mean to laugh, but that's some picture you just painted. And I could tell it hurt.*

She sighed heavily. *It did.*

Was it possible another witch or warlock had messed with her spell? Some of the covens were deep into dark magic and she was so untried, she had no clue what she was doing. *Vaughn, what if it was Loghry?*

He didn't respond right away but continued to rub her back gently. *Maybe he's been hunting for you through his spellcasting ability and found you.*

I suppose it's possible, but this is uncharted territory for me. She squeezed her eyes shut and once more opened up to her power. Reluctantly, she focused on Loghry, but she needed to figure out what happened.

As she reviewed the moment her foray into the future got disrupted, she could feel the nature of the magic that attacked her. It felt very male, not a witch at all. And it felt old, as in it had been around for a while.

Recognition and understanding arrived. Emma could see what Loghry had done. First, he'd disabled her ability to see the future, then he'd sent a mountain of pain to force her out of her spell completely. She could almost taste the nature of his dark magic.

Vaughn, it was Loghry. I'm sure of it now.

That doesn't surprise either of us, does it?

Not even a little.

From her sitting position as she leaned against Vaughn, she was able to see the ghosts. They were finally moving around better.

Becca, were you hurt?

She shook her head. *We can't feel pain, but we felt shut down, unable to move or even to see for a long time. We're all okay, but what happened?*

She explained about Loghry.

Becca's expression grew grim. *I am soooo not surprised. He's a monster.*

Emma couldn't have agreed more.

All three ghosts hovered in the air, watching her. They were so lovely and wore the same outfits, which helped Emma to know which one was Becca. She was still sporting her jeans and red tank top.

Many ghosts stuck around for a while, especially those killed in a violent way. She suspected Becca and her sisters needed some sort of closure before they could pass permanently to the next life. Maybe they even needed to help get Loghry.

So, when do we leave?

What do you mean?

To rescue these girls, of course. I can see the clock above your couch and it's only 11:15. The driver of the truck spoke about having arrived just before midnight. You and Officer Vaughn have plenty of time to save the girls.

Emma drew back from Vaughn's embrace then rose to her feet.

He stood up along with her, but met her gaze, frowning heavily. "What's wrong, Em? What's going on now? Did you see more of the images?"

She met his gaze. "I think we have a job to do, but it doesn't involve Loghry, at least not directly. We need to go to Savage Territory.

"Savage? You're kidding."

Emma relayed the movie-like images to him, of the truck transporting teens through wolf territory. She was also explicit about the ghosts and what Becca had suggested they do next.

When she heard glass clinking on the hutch, she leaned around Vaughn. "Hey, girls, don't mess with the canisters."

Vaughn turned as well. "What the hell?"

"What?" Emma wondered if he could see something she couldn't.

"I don't know how this is possible, but I can see the triplets. This is weird. Vampires don't usually see ghosts. And I definitely couldn't before."

"Then how are you doing it now?"

"I have no idea. And they're wearing clothes, each of them, or what looks like clothes."

Emma's brows rose. "Yeah, that was actually the first thing they did. They got dressed, probably for my sake."

Becca intruded. *Emma, please tell Vaughn that we need to get going. We've already wasted three minutes. Tick-tock.*

She turned to look at Vaughn. "Becca says we need to get the girls."

He jerked his chin in the direction of the hutch. "Will they be with us?"

"Of course. Looks like we're a team. All of us."

"So let me get this straight. You and me and three ghosts, are supposed to chase down a delivery truck, deep in Savage Territory, and rescue these girls?"

"Sure. Why not? I mean what else do we have to do? Besides, this is the series of images that came to me even though I focused on Loghry and his mansion. I think we should do it."

He stared at her for a long moment. She could see the wheels turning. "And I have a contact on Savage Border Patrol, an officer I trust, who would like nothing more than to disrupt the trafficking in his territory. Officer Fergus, do you know him?"

Emma shook her head. "I never knew a lot of shifters. Max kept his relationship with me separate. But there's something I forgot to tell you."

"What?"

She held his gaze firmly, then smiled. "The storage unit facility belongs to Loghry."

He smiled as well. "So there it is."

"Yep, there it is."

"Then, let's do it."

CHAPTER FOUR

While Emma armed up, Vaughn stood on the patio outside the master bedroom and used his cell to contact Officer Eric Fergus of the Savage Territory Border Patrol. Fergus was the alpha of one of the most powerful packs in Savage. Among wolf leadership, he held a lot of sway.

Vaughn had barely gotten two words out when Fergus said he was in. He'd do whatever Vaughn needed him to do to rescue the girls. He'd heard about the set-up in the Graveyard and was glad to learn Vaughn and Emma had made it out alive.

The mention of Loghry's storage unit facility had the wolf growling. "That bastard. I hope I get the chance one day to take him down. He puts spells on our female shifters and they disappear into his sex clubs until they're broken. Those who find their way back to Savage, take years to recover."

Vaughn made arrangements to meet Fergus in fifteen minutes at the forest edge near the storage facility. Fergus would bring two of his best men as well as a backup force. "In the meantime, I'm headed to Crescent for weapons."

"Good. See you in a few." Fergus had a gruff voice and was muscled as hell. Vaughn could count on him to see the mission through.

He checked his Glock then secured it back in its holster. As he was putting his phone into the pocket of his jeans, Emma emerged from the house. She had her sidearm in place, her shoulders squared. He held his hand out to her. "Ready for this?"

Emma smiled crookedly. "Hell, yeah." She patted her Sig Sauer.

When she climbed up on his right boot, he pulled her tight against him. He took her into the air, flying north in the direction of Crescent Territory. Lily had already called him back to let him know that Brannick had changed locations. Apparently, the safe house was no longer safe, and he would meet Vaughn in the alley behind his favorite Chinese restaurant, not far from the Border Patrol station.

Vaughn flew high in the air to avoid detection by any low flyers or anyone on the lookout for either Emma or himself.

Emma kept watch as well and more than once alerted him to a Crescent officer hovering near the rooftops of buildings they passed over. He also kept his shielding mechanism active. If Loghry happened to be in the area, he wouldn't be able to see Vaughn, or even Emma, because of Vaughn's shield.

His cloaking ability wouldn't make him invisible to vampires, however, so that when he finally descended into the alley behind the restaurant, Brannick saw him right away. He offered a slow dip of his chin.

His gaze went to Emma. "Is this the witch you told me about, the one you helped rescue those girls?"

"Yes." He introduced Emma but wasn't surprised when Brannick kept his distance.

The vampire had a hard look with dark brown hair combed straight back. His green eyes always looked pinched. He had deep lines beside his mouth and rarely smiled. He was clean as a whistle in terms of corruption and was known for his cool head. But rage simmered within Brannick, evidenced by the frequent flare of his nostrils.

Fate had delivered a series of hard blows to Brannick, more than any of Vaughn's fellow officers. He'd lost his pregnant wife and a young daughter to the *alter* nightmare thirteen years ago when a tainted supply of a brand name soft drink had been corrupted with vampire serum.

Enraged, he'd tried to punish the cartels for all the ways they worked to create more *alters* in the human portion of Phoenix.

Both Connor and Vaughn had tried to warn Brannick. But fury

had fueled his vendetta. In turn, the cartels had targeted his extended family. His parents had been killed and his sister trafficked and sold to a dark witch coven in Elegance. She'd been used as a human sacrifice, something Brannick had been forced to witness.

He'd pulled in his vengeance, but he'd had a lot of grief to deal with afterward. The truth was, they all did. No one came to Five Bridges without having suffered severe losses. Every pregnant woman who went through the *alter* lost her baby, no exceptions. Fetuses and children couldn't survive the horrendous changes the *alter* metamorphosis created, no matter which of the five species the human became, whether vampire or spellcaster, shifter, fae, or dead-talker.

A loud explosion hit the air, though probably a good mile away. Vaughn turned in the direction from which the blast had come. "What the hell was that?"

Brannick gestured toward the west. "Five Bridges is expanding. According to the latest stats, we've added five thousand *alters* in the past ten months. Unprecedented numbers. The U.S. finally agreed to give us another square mile off Crescent and Revel Territories then another square mile off Elegance in the east and Savage to the south."

As if on cue, a second but even more distant explosion sounded toward Savage Territory. "That'll make the shifters happy. They've wanted to plant more trees. Now they can."

"Speaking of Savage, we've got to get going. Did you bring what I asked for?"

"Not exactly."

Vaughn scowled. "What does that mean? We've only got a few minutes to get over there." Going into Savage Territory, they had to have weapons. Wolves were vicious fighters and probably the best-equipped with illegal firearms. But they protected their supply.

Brannick's nostrils flared. "It means I'm coming with. Simple as that. No argument. I've sat on the sidelines way too long and after the stunt Loghry pulled in the Graveyard, well, let's just say my patience has finally worn thin. If I can help save some teenage girls tonight, I'm going to do just that."

There were barely a handful of moments since Vaughn's *alter* when he experienced a profound gratitude. Right now, knowing Brannick would throw in with them when he knew damn well he and Emma had a price on their heads, meant everything to Vaughn.

He extended his hand to Brannick who gripped him at the forearm in a solid hold. Vaughn returned the favor.

Vaughn nodded. "All right then. We're headed deep into Savage." He checked his internal clock, that critical biological timepiece all vampires had which ensured they stayed well away from the rising sun. But it also told him the exact time no matter the hour, day or night.

It was eleven-thirty and they needed to move out now.

Brannick opened the duffel and handed him an AR-15. Knowing Emma couldn't levitate, Brannick shouldered the duffel and rose slowly into the air.

He hit Vaughn's telepathy. *Let me see what's up here before you pass the roofline.*

Good plan.

With Emma once more glued to his side and both her relatively small feet planted on his right boot, he began to levitate in Brannick's direction, but stayed just below the roofs of the adjacent buildings.

As soon as Brannick waved him up, Vaughn hit the sky fast, speeding straight up then swinging southwest toward Savage.

Brannick took up a wing position on Vaughn's left. From Vaughn's peripheral, he could see the triplets, each keeping pace a little ahead of him and to the right. Not exactly the kind of black ops force needed to rescue half a dozen teens but it would do. Being armed helped. He had his AR-15 looped over his left shoulder.

Emma guided them into the central forest of Savage and soon enough he spotted the delivery truck. It was almost at its destination. *Is that the one?*

Yep. That's it. I recognize the logo on the back. Willow Creek Office Furniture.

Seeing that the forest line stopped, Vaughn veered to the right away from the truck. The shifters were waiting for them at the point where the pines gave way to a broad vacant lot, which in turn led to the storage units. Fortunately, there were few other buildings around, most having been bulldozed and the ground left to grow desert weeds.

Adrenaline pumped through Vaughn's system and his fangs thrummed in his mouth as he headed for Fergus and his men. Descending gradually, he slowed to land a few feet from Fergus. The powerful shifter wore his thick, black hair like a mane past his shoulders and braided on one side.

Fergus lifted his own AR-15 in greeting. Two more shifters flanked him, each rough-looking. All three belonged to the Savage Border Patrol, but faced the same issues that his own force endured. Like the other territories, at least half the Savage ranks were corrupt, just like Crescent and Elegance.

Fergus greeted Vaughn and inclined his head to Emma. Vaughn eased Emma off his foot then introduced her.

For a moment, Fergus's jaw worked as he stared at Emma. Vaughn bristled. He didn't know what the hell Fergus was thinking, but he looked angry. In response, Vaughn took Emma's hand.

He was about to step in front of Emma to protect her, when Fergus inclined his head toward her and held it as if bowing to her. He stayed in this position for at least ten seconds. "You are welcome in my forest, Emma Delacey. Max was one of my best friends. I'm alpha to the Gordion Pack." He gestured with a wave of his arm to the forest line. "This is our domain."

Vaughn glanced in the direction of the pines and to his astonishment watched at least two dozen shifters emerge from places of camouflage. They also bowed to Emma.

She lifted her chin and nodded, then spoke in a clear voice. "I wish I'd had the chance to know those Max valued and loved."

Fergus scowled, grinding his jaw again. "His death was tragic, another wrong I'd like to right. You have but to ask anything of me, Emma, and I'm yours to command."

Vaughn knew he gripped Emma's hand harder than he should, but Fergus had a lot of presence and was unmated. Emma had already fallen in love with a shifter once before. The thought she could fall for this one, raised his hackles.

Fergus turned his attention back to Vaughn. "Where do you want us?"

Vaughn drew a deep breath and switched gears. "Did you see the truck arrive?"

"We did, and I can hear it right now." Fergus gestured with a toss of his hand toward the distant block wall topped with barbed wire. "It's heading down the alley just as you said it would. So, how do you want to do this?"

"I'll let Emma tell you what she saw."

Emma kept her voice low as she talked about the number of girls in the truck, six in all, the warlocks in charge, the fat shifter in the office, as well as the two guards in the facility. "But the images scrambled at that point, which means I can't be sure how many we'll be facing. There could be more guards in the facility or some in the strip-center building. We won't really know til we get in there."

"Doesn't matter." Fergus's lips turned down. "We'll deal with whatever we find." He gestured to the ground at his feet.

Vaughn saw that he'd drawn a rough map.

"The complex has an exit here." He tapped his foot on the western edge. "And one that leads at the back onto the southernmost street. The alley is right there, fifty yards away. It ends at the desert. Do you see it?"

Vaughn nodded. "Yes."

"My men will come in from the western exit, in wolf form initially. You come in from the front and we'll see what happens." Vaughn didn't know a whole lot about the shifter experience except that battle and transforming into wolves went hand-in-hand, a necessity of their *alter* condition.

Vaughn nodded. Emma met his gaze and dipped her chin once. Brannick did the same.

The teams split up. Vaughn watched as each of the shifters, with barely a thought, moved fluidly into their wolf form then loped across the open land to the west of the storage facility. He wasn't sure where their weapons went, but apparently part of the shifter ability was transforming everything they held or wore into their wolfness.

Within a matter of seconds, they'd disappeared.

He was about to hold out his arm to Emma, when he realized she was levitating. Stunned, he gripped her arm, fearing she'd fall.

But she smiled at him. "I'm okay. I've picked this up from you, Vaughn. I don't know what's going on between us, but right now I can levitate as though I've been doing it my entire life. I must have gained the skill from you, and it rocks."

She didn't wait for him, either, but rose in the air and sped in the direction of the alley. He caught up with her, stunned.

Brannick flew on the opposite side of her. He caught Vaughn's gaze. *What the hell? Did you know she could fly?*

He shook his head. *Had no idea.*

Something strange is going on between the pair of you.

I know.

The ghosts appeared and flew near Emma. He felt it as well, just as Emma had said. They were a team.

Her voice entered his mind. *Let's save us some girls.*

~ ~ ~

Emma couldn't believe she was five feet off the ground, tracking toward the alley. She knew some of the most powerful spellcasters could levitate, but she'd never been able to. When Vaughn had moved her off his boot, however, for a few seconds she'd found herself suspended in the air if only an inch above the ground.

After she'd met Officer Fergus and received his warm, respectful greeting, she'd done some surreptitious practicing. Stranger still was the sure knowledge the new ability came fully formed.

She knew she'd be able to fly with Vaughn's skill, so she did.

Of course the real question surfaced almost immediately as in why she could suddenly do this remarkable thing. But she had no answer. Her instincts, however, leaned toward her growing relationship with Vaughn.

They'd crossed a critical threshold in the past few hours and their new-found intimacy seemed to be having an effect on them both. Vaughn could see the ghosts and he'd played a role in her spellroom that allowed Emma to find the future.

As she, Vaughn and Brannick turned into the alley, the Willow Creek truck was already backing into the storage facility. The obese shifter was waving his arms in a loose manner. "Keep going."

Vaughn shot forward, rifle in hand, and called out, "I've got a better idea. Shut it down. Now."

The slovenly shifter reached behind his back and drew his pistol. Vaughn whipped in his direction and fired once. The shifter fell, shot through the chest.

Vaughn levitated toward the truck. By then, the two warlocks had their hands in the air, the engine off.

Emma flew with Brannick above the wall separating the alley from the storage facility, weapons aimed at the two security guards she'd seen in the stream of images. They'd started moving in the direction of the truck, AR-15s at hip level.

Brannick's deep voice hit the air. "Drop your weapons. Now."

The two guards glanced, up then immediately set their rifles on the asphalt.

Emma called out. "On the ground. Face down. Both of you."

Brannick turned to her. "Keep your weapons on these two. I'll open the truck."

"I've got a better idea."

A smile spread over his face, and he nodded. "You gonna kill em?"

"Not quite, but I'm tempted. What I want to do, once we're finished here, is haul them to the Trib jail."

Brannick looked skeptical, but she wasn't about to start explaining her position. She knew that even if she booked them at the Tribunal, their bosses would get them released in a short period of time. But building a decent society in Five Bridges had to start somewhere.

Emma levitated down to the asphalt. She touched the first guard on the back of the skull. He started to move, but Emma released a small portion of her energy, knocking the warlock out. She moved to the other guard.

"Don't kill me." He laced his hands at the base of his neck.

But Emma didn't need to reach the more vulnerable location to render him unconscious. The man panicked, however, and started to roll when she drew close. She jumped on his back, pinning him to the ground. Though he tried to protect his head with both hands, the moment she made contact with his skull and her energy flowed, his body went limp. He'd be asleep for a long time.

Fergus and the wolves arrived just as she was dusting off her jeans. They changed swiftly back to their much more human, forms.

"Nice work, Emma." Fergus's rough voice flowed over her. He glanced at his men. "Let's help Brannick with the girls."

Seeing that there was plenty of support for getting the teens out of the truck, Emma moved around the front where Vaughn covered the warlocks.

She wiggled her fingers in the air. "Let me take care of them so we can help Brannick and the others get the girls out of here."

Vaughn's lips curved. "Sounds good to me." He jerked the door open.

The driver glanced at her hand. "You'd do that to one of your own kind?"

Was he really playing the warlock card?

Emma made a disgusted sound at the back of her throat. "You may be a spellcaster, but you're not one of my kind. You're a piece of garbage."

Emma hopped on the running board. "I should kill you right now for trafficking these girls, but that's not my job. Instead, we'll be taking you to the Trib for trial."

When the warlock smiled because everyone knew any kind of Tribunal justice was a sham, she added, "But I'm giving you a warning. Get out of this business or if I ever find you running humans again, I'll kill you on sight and that's a promise. Right now, if you resist what I'm about to do, or try to hurt me, Officer Vaughn will shoot. Now lean forward on the steering wheel."

He all but collapsed.

"Vaughn, cover his friend who's eyeing me with real hatred right now."

"Bitch-witch," the warlock muttered.

"Oh, I've never heard that one before. Now, lift your hands and keep your eye on Officer Vaughn."

The moment he turned to face Vaughn, she reached in and zapped the driver. He stayed where he was, though now he was slumped over the wheel in a deep sleep.

She rounded the truck and was ready to perform her magic a fourth time, but to her surprise, Vaughn opened the door and jerked the warlock out of the cab. From the high perch of the truck bench, he fell a tidy distance and landed hard on the asphalt.

He lay on his stomach, blood oozing from his nose and mouth. Vaughn planted a boot on the warlock's back. "Don't you ever call a Tribunal Public Safety officer a 'bitch', do you understand?"

"Yes, sir."

Emma dipped down and zapped him as well.

With both men out, she headed to the back of the truck. Vaughn joined her. Brannick already had the doors open and was handing the girls down to the shifters.

Fergus and his men each had a girl in his arms. Vaughn was about to take one of them when the triplets started flying wildly over their heads, sweeping back and forth.

Vaughn was watching them as well. "What's with our ghosts?"

"Not sure. Let me find out."

She switched to telepathy. *Becca, what's going on?*

Loghry. He's here. And he's got some men with him. She turned to face south. *That way. The other side of the street, though quite a ways off.* She pointed in a southeasterly direction toward the main road.

So much for bringing these criminals to the Trib.

How far away?

Not far, but I don't know distance. Just hurry.

"Becca said Loghry's here, coming from the southeast beyond the main road. He's not alone."

Vaughn lifted the last of the girls out, and Brannick jumped to the ground. Vaughn rose swiftly in the air, then returned as fast.

"Loghry, incoming with twenty, all warlocks and armed, all levitating. Now, let's get these girls out of here."

The shifter closest to Emma turned to her. "Take this girl. She's very thin and hardly weighs anything. You'll be able to levitate her out."

Emma nodded. She took the girl by the hand and with a few words, arranged the teen against her side. With an arm around her waist and holding her snug, she rose into the air. The funny thing was, the girl felt light as a feather, which meant she was experiencing Vaughn's physical vampire strength.

Incredible.

Frightened by being suddenly airborne, the girl screamed and threw both arms around Emma.

"You're doing fine, just hold on tight. But we've gotta go."

The shifter inclined his head to Emma. The more powerful wolves could levitate as well as change into their phenomenal running shapes. Right now, with a frightened human in his arms, the shifter levitated and moved fast. She kept up with him, following in his wake two feet above the asphalt.

The shifter headed toward the end of the row of storage units, then banked down the long row that extended all the way to the back of the complex. With Loghry in pursuit, she saw the wisdom of staying hidden within the complex. Unless the wizard and his men were in a direct line with the row, they wouldn't be able to see them. The problem, of course, was getting out of the facility.

She heard Brannick's deep voice shouting behind her. "Faster, Emma."

She kept her head below the roofline but increased her speed.

She heard gunfire.

Where was Vaughn?

Brannick, another girl in his arms, now levitated on one side of her. "We're heading into the forest. We'll lose Loghry and his men in there. The back-up force will take over for us as soon as we start across the open field."

Adrenaline flooded her body, and her heart pounded with energy and intent. The girl she held clung to her, shaking.

Brannick stuck close, and as they neared the end of the facility, he said, "We'll go to the right, up and over, then back low to the ground for cover. Ready?"

"Yes."

"On my mark. Now!"

Emma veered to the right alongside Brannick, then flew up to the roof. A staccato of gunfire sounded. She felt a bullet whiz by.

She cleared the roof and immediately descended to a foot above the ground out of the line of fire. She saw the first shifter with the girl in his arms, dart into the forest. She had Vaughn's ability now and didn't hold back. She rushed forward so fast, she surprised herself. Aiming for the opening, she ignored the prolonged sound of gunfire coming from behind her.

Brannick stuck right with her as well.

Several shifters moved into the open field to cover them and were levitating and firing into the air. The noise soon became deafening.

The moment she made it into the dark cover of the pine trees, she began to slow, though she kept flying down the path to give room to those behind her.

She saw the original girl and shifter. She headed toward them, dropping off to the side as she slowed to a stop.

When she had her feet on the ground, the girl clinging to her neck slowly unwound her arms. She had a heavy bruise on her cheek, a sign of either the ride in the truck or how badly she'd been treated.

"Are we safe here?" How young her voice sounded. Emma winced. She couldn't be more than twelve or thirteen.

"Yes. Don't worry. You're among friends. You'll be home within a couple more hours. Okay?"

The girl's eyes were wide. She wrapped her arms around her stomach. "Okay." She sat down beside the other girl on a thick bank of pine needles.

Brannick settled his girl there as well. The rest followed in a quick wave until all six were once more huddled together. The girl who had been unconscious had awakened but looked dazed.

Brannick gestured to Fergus. "Do you and your pack have a way to get these girls back to their families?"

Fergus looked around and answered quietly, "We do."

"Tell me."

"We've got tunnels we can use, but I'm thinking we should go within the next few minutes. We already know what Loghry does when his product is stolen from him."

Brannick glanced at the girls. "Make it happen."

When Fergus got on the phone, the ghosts caught Emma's attention once more, only she didn't sense danger this time. Instead, they flew above the young women, swaying back and forth and smiling. She felt their celebration and would have levitated to join them, but the human girls were already in a state of shock.

She merely blew kisses to Becca and her sisters.

She glanced back up the path, in the direction she'd entered the forest. She then turned in a circle because she didn't see Vaughn.

All the girls were here now, including the one Vaughn had carried in his arms. This meant someone else had transported her the rest of the way.

Emma headed in the direction of the now faint gunfire. From a distance, she could see that the shifters were still engaged in a shoot-out, but Vaughn was nowhere in sight.

She moved off the path where the fighting was heaviest. In a quiet voice, she made her presence known to those Savage Border Patrol officers who made up part of the reserve force. "I'm looking for one of the Crescent Border Patrol officers."

The nearest shifter gestured to the left of the path. "Over there, Ma'am. He's been shot."

Her heart fell so hard, she nearly stumbled. She was going to ask if he was dead, but that's when she caught sight of him. He was on the ground, flat on his back and breathing, thank God.

She could see he was in a lot of pain. He had an arm slung over his forehead and his lips were a tight line.

Vaughn?

His arm dropped away, and he looked around until he saw her. She crouched as she moved toward him. The tree line was only twenty feet away. A stray bullet could catch her if she wasn't careful.

When he saw her, he continued telepathically. *Emma, thank God you're okay.*

She looked at his bloody leg. It was torn up bad, the jeans cut away. She could see bone.

You should have called for me.

I didn't want you to see this.

At that, she laughed. "Why the hell not? I've seen worse. I've treated worse."

A shifter medic was opening his pack, but she stopped him. "I'll take care of this."

He nodded, then moved to one of his own who leaned up against a tree holding his arm.

Emma didn't address the leg right away. Instead, she put her hand on Vaughn's forehead. "This should help."

~ ~ ~

Vaughn was about to say, 'What will help', when a drug-like wave moved into his head, and his whole body relaxed. He knew he was in pain yet felt separated from it at the same time.

Which was a good thing, since he could feel Emma now pushing into the wound. A stream of hot pain sliced through the feel-good, and his mind went on an agonizing roller-coaster ride. He was pretty sure he was going to pass out.

Then everything disappeared.

When he regained consciousness, he could feel a profound pressure on his leg. The pain had become a dull pounding in his skull, but not impossible to bear. Emma must have set his leg.

The pop of weapon-fire had disappeared, which meant the battle was over. There was also a lot of male laughter coming from different directions.

It sounded so familiar, the way he and his vampire brothers-in-arms would be after a significant battle. He heard friendly shouting as well. Men were the same everywhere, including in Five Bridges, whether you were a vampire or a shifter.

"How are the girls?" His voice sounded slurred.

"Ah, you're awake. Good. They're fine. When I left Fergus to find you, he was making arrangements to get them out of here right away."

He lifted up enough so that he could see what she was doing. She had both hands covering the wound. Healing flowed into his skin, muscle and bone. The bullet had caught his calf from behind and gone through the shinbone in front. Yeah, it had hurt like hell. "They got a tunnel?" The ever industrious cartels had built dozens of tunnels that went under the pavement and ended in cartel owned homes on the human side of Phoenix. Eventually, other tunnels were built by the decent citizens of Five Bridges to get humans back to safety.

Emma met his gaze and smiled that quirky smile of hers, the way she looked when she was pleased with something. "They've got several. I think they might even be taking them through now."

"Seriously?"

"Shifters don't mess around."

"That's right. Max."

"You remind me of him, Vaughn. You're a man of purpose and action. He was, too."

He felt conflicted. He liked the compliment, but he'd started feeling jealous of a man long dead.

He glanced down at the wound. "It doesn't hurt anymore."

She sat back on her heels. "Good. But just so you know, I've never had this kind of healing gift before, at least not at this level. And I'm levitating now as well as possessing more natural strength. It was so easy to carry that girl in my arms while levitating. Anything new and unusual you want to report?"

He understood what she was getting at. "Well, the ghosts are looking more real to me by the minute, and I've never flown as I did getting the last girl back here. Even when I got hit, I speared the sky and shot into the forest like a rocket." He might be bragging a little, but he didn't care.

She scooted closer and took his hand. "What's going on here, Vaughn? It's so strange. I mean, I can levitate, for God's sake. But it was more than that. I had your skill level as though being with you, maybe as part of the spell I'd created, transferred your ability to me."

He stroked her face. "I don't know, but I think it rocks, because we just saved six young teens from one of the most hellish experiences in Five Bridges."

She smiled. "We did, didn't we?" She then leaned down and put her lips on his.

Desire rose quickly, which meant he had to quit as in right now. He drew back.

"What is it? You still in pain?" She looked worried.

A smile took over his lips. "Sort of, but not my leg this time."

She stared at him for a moment. Then her brows rose, and she giggled. Again that quirk of a smile made an appearance. Her voice entered his head. *Got it. No public kissing.*

Not after a win, and not when I'm on my back and you look so beautiful. Besides, I don't know what you did to my head, but I'm feeling pumped.

You mean when I put my hand on your forehead?

Yeah.

I hate to break it to you, Vaughn, but it's a form of my witch killing power.

He sat up way too fast. "What?"

Since he'd spoken in a loud voice, several Savage Border Patrol officers turned in his direction. All the officers, both male and female, eyed Emma with suspicion. Shifters had the same problem with witches. He apologized for the outburst and everyone went back to their conversations.

She lowered her voice. "Yes, I could have zapped you good. But first I'd have to actually load that kind of charge into my fingers and for some inexplicable reason, as in you mean a helluva lot to me, I didn't want to do that. Don't you trust me, Vaughn?"

He rose to his feet and shook out his legs. When she stood up as well, he took her shoulders in his hands. "I do trust you. I was surprised, that's all. I'm still getting use to your witch gifts."

He glanced around once more and afterward checked his sidearm. He drew his Glock from his holster then returned it. This particular habit stuck with all peace officers, making sure your weapons were in order.

As for the AR-15, it was probably with Fergus's forces and they were welcome to it for the service the troops had performed tonight. "How about we find Fergus and Brannick, see if they need us? If not, I'm thinking I'd like to take you home."

"Sounds good."

When he turned toward the main path, it would have been a natural time to let go of her hand, but he didn't want to. Instead, he felt a primal need to make a show of it. He saw the way many of the shifter males looked at Emma, like something they wanted to devour. And he never lost sight of the fact she'd once loved an alpha.

~ ~ ~

Emma's heart rate soared, but it had nothing to do with fear. Instead, she couldn't believe Vaughn hadn't released her hand. In the *alter* world, it was a clear signal that he thought of her as his woman and every other man present should back off.

She didn't miss how many gazes slid to their joined hands as they walked by. A lot of the men even took a small step back as a result.

Shifters were generally a gregarious bunch and many of them congratulated both Vaughn and herself for setting up and taking part in the rescue.

Vaughn asked one of the shifters where Fergus was and got directions that involved taking a side detour. The destination proved to be a large rowdy bar about a mile distant from the storage unit site.

She and Vaughn found Brannick in the center of the bar standing beside Fergus, laughing with him. The men were about the same massive size as Vaughn, though slightly shorter and each almost as handsome.

The first thing she did was ask for an update. "What happened with the gun battle? Did any of Loghry and his crew get hit? I mean, I'd love to hear that Loghry got shot out of the sky. Nothing would make me happier."

Fergus shook his head. "No such luck. A couple of his warlocks went down. I had my men haul them to the morgue. But a general consensus among my pack is that Loghry initiated some kind of spell for himself. A black cloud hung over the storage facility, blocking out the night sky in that direction. Once the shooting stopped, the cloud and Loghry were gone. Wish I had better news for you."

Emma sighed then shrugged. "It was too much to hope for, but the girls are all safe?"

At that, Fergus smiled. "All safe and headed home."

"Well that's the only important news anyway. And thanks again, Fergus and Brannick, for being part of this. I'm more grateful than I can possibly express."

Both men nodded. Vaughn squeezed her hand and smiled down at her, his eyes warm with affection.

"So what do you think of this place?" Fergus swept his hand to encompass the shifter hang-out.

"I think it's great. Elegance doesn't have nearly enough clubs or bars that bring its people together just for fun." That was the exact truth. Most of the clubs serviced the sex trade and the humans who arrived in droves nightly to take advantage of it. Five Bridges had a long way to go.

The bar had a large sand pit in the center designed for pack challenges when a male wanted to make a bid for alpha status. But it was also used for public fist fights and occasionally full-on wolf fang battles, both of which shifters loved to participate in and watch. Max had told her about them and had hoped, once he got his pack used to her as his mate, to take her to see one.

As Vaughn entered a spirited conversation with Fergus and Brannick, her memories grew clouded with her time as Max's chosen mate. She'd loved the big wolf. She'd felt such guilt that he'd died the way he did, ambushed when he'd returned from a long weekend at her home. He'd barely crossed the bridge into Savage Territory when he'd been shot and killed.

"Hello, Emma. How are you?"

Emma recognized the raspy wolf voice and a shudder ran through her.

Dagen.

He'd spoken quietly, and she suspected his intention was to make sure Vaughn didn't hear him.

Still holding Vaughn's hand, she pivoted slightly toward the alpha who had taken over Max's pack. Vaughn stayed put since he was still engaged in what sounded like a loud though friendly debate with Fergus.

Dagen stood a couple of feet away, flanked by two of his powerful pack-mates. Emma now stood at a right-angle to Vaughn. Very clever of the wolf.

"You know what I think about you, Dagen. There's no need for small talk, so why don't you and your friends just move along."

He spoke in a low voice. "You've always misunderstood me. I've protected you in ways you can't even imagine. I merely wanted to congratulate you. I heard about the good deed you and your vampire friend just accomplished." He lifted a bottle of beer to her. When his gaze fell to her hand still held in Vaughn's warm clasp, his eyes darkened and his lips turned down.

She couldn't get over the feeling Dagen had always thought of her as belonging to him. It made no sense, yet she could feel his anger.

He was a bit shorter than Max had been, and fell a couple of inches shy of Vaughn. But Dagen had powerful shoulders and arms, exposed by a leather jacket with the sleeves cut off and dotted with at least two dozen spiked silver studs. He worked out and it showed. He didn't have an ounce of fat on his lean, muscled body.

He had dark ferret-like eyes always on the move. He wore his blackish brown hair in a Mohawk, his scalp on the sides shaved clean and bearing a series of skull tattoos along the space above each ear.

He had a lot of charisma and women went for him. He wore black leathers treated with the same spiked studs down the outer seams. Steel-toed boots made a horrific promise to anyone falling during a mano-a-mano battle with him.

He lifted the bottle to his lips and took a swig.

Dagen had made a play for her after Max died, but she'd never had the smallest interest in the shifter. He was all sleaze, and she knew in her gut he was the one who had assassinated Max.

When Vaughn turned toward her, Dagen moved a few feet away, his beta guards with him.

Vaughn's grip tightened on her hand. "That's Dagen, isn't it?"

"Yep, that's him."

"He looks different with the Mohawk, but I remember him from when I was hunting for my sister. What did he say to you?"

She switched to telepathy. Shifters had excellent hearing, and she didn't want her conversation with Vaughn reported by anyone eavesdropping. *Would you believe he wanted to congratulate us on rescuing the girls?*

Like he gives a shit.

Exactly.

Dagen stood a few yards distant. He was still watching her, but he hadn't yet made eye-contact with Vaughn. When he did, it wouldn't be good.

Vaughn growled softly, a very *alter* kind of sound. *He's after you, Em. I can smell it from here.*

I know he is, but I've never understood why. It's like he's obsessed. Maybe he thinks that because I was with Max, I should belong to him now, sort of an alpha thing.

Whatever it is, he's pissing me off.

She felt the tension in his body and because of it, she turned toward him, which forced Vaughn to focus on her.

Listen to me. If you start something here, you'll have to finish it in a one-on-one fight. She inclined her head toward the sand pit. *You don't want to do that. Dagen won't battle with honor, and he'll kill you if he can.*

She saw that Vaughn's fangs were low on his lips. *Sorry, Em, but it may not be up to me.*

The entire tenor of the room changed in a heartbeat.

The predatory wolf energy Dagen emitted as he now glared at Vaughn, brought his pack moving closer to him. In addition, the swell of male energy radiating from Vaughn alerted all the testosterone in the room a fight was in the making.

Dagen sauntered closer, moving to stand in front of Emma once more. He grimaced as he looked Vaughn up and down.

"So, what do you think, Emma? Could this vampire beat me in the pit?"

"Go to hell, Dagen. We're not here to fight."

He shifted his gaze to Emma. "I don't know why you're pissed at me. I was ready to take you as my mistress, to be seen with you even though you're a witch and some of my pack wouldn't approve."

She could feel Vaughn bristling and knew how badly this could end. So, she did the only sensible thing she could think of.

She drew her right fist back and slugged Dagen as hard as she could, square on the jaw. What she hadn't counted on was an increased physical capacity that felt more vampire than witch.

Holy shit! She watched Dagen's head snap back, he lost his footing, slammed against a table, then slid to the floor. The whole room emitted a collective gasp.

For a long moment, Emma was startled. But she collected herself quickly, knowing she needed to follow up her assault with a few carefully chosen words. "Leave me alone, Dagen. Max was the only shifter I wanted, and he's dead. Now I'm with Vaughn, a Crescent Border Patrol officer I respect and admire, so get over yourself."

Brannick moved to stand next to Vaughn, while Fergus drew close to Emma. She could feel Fergus's pack moving in to support their alpha just as Dagen's pack had started gathering behind him.

Emma felt the situation teeter on the brink of disaster, but the last thing she wanted was a bar brawl on her account.

Dagen's eyes glittered as he stared up at her. When he rose to his feet, Fergus took a couple of steps forward, not quite blocking her from Dagen, but close. "We don't want trouble, Dagen. Not with so much to celebrate. Emma made her decision clear to you five years ago, and I need you to back off. *Now*." The last word carried a kind of wolf-strength that resounded through the space.

Emma watched as the shifters all over the bar continued to align into packs, some moving in support of Dagen, others closing in around Fergus, very typical of Savage.

But why did Dagen have to start something?

Vaughn hadn't moved either. He stood rigid beside Emma, his hands in tight fists. The vampire was ready to fight.

Finally, Dagen slid his gaze from Emma to Fergus. He squared his shoulders. "I've disrupted things tonight. And I apologize. Everyone knows I've cared about Emma, because I should have been there to protect Max. I meant no disrespect."

Liar. He was such a liar. She wanted to hit him again.

Emma shook with hatred for the man. He might be respected because of his alpha status, but he was pure evil. He embodied the psychotic quality that had sunk Five Bridges into a nightmare in the first place.

Suddenly, the triplets appeared, though moving higher in the air. Becca waved at Emma but she looked distressed. *What is it, Becca?*

Dagen. We just discovered he has a connection to Loghry. He might even be working for him.

Loghry and Dagen. Sounded like a match made in hell.

Thanks for letting me know.

She squeezed Vaughn's hand. *Did you see Becca just now?*

Yes. She didn't look very happy.

Vaughn, she thinks Dagen might be working for Loghry. We need to get the hell out of here.

Let's do it.

Aloud she said, "I'm ready to head home."

He slid his arm around her waist. "Then we should go."

Emma glanced at Dagen. He wore an arrested expression on his face, almost calculating. She saw his hand slide into his pants pocket. He turned his back on Emma, but she watched him pull his phone to his ear.

Yep, Dagen and Loghry.

Vaughn, Dagen's on his phone.

I see him. I've already told Brannick what's going on. He's talking to Fergus now, getting a plan together to get us out of Savage. We won't be able to fly out. Brannick and I both agree that Loghry and his men could still be up there waiting for us.

Couldn't we fly using your disguising shield?

We don't want to take the chance that Loghry has a vampire in his employ. A vampire would see through the shield.

Okay. Got it.

I'll fill you in as soon as I hear back.

Fergus led the way out of the bar, his phone to his ear as well. He spoke quietly, his gaze moving back and forth, always checking the terrain. Brannick brought up the rear.

The shifters belonging to Fergus's Gordion Pack had lined up protectively on either side of the path to the door. They were ready to do battle if needed.

She didn't really take a decent breath until she was outside and Vaughn telepathically relayed Fergus's plan to get them out of the territory by way of a van. They would need to move swiftly through the forest first to avoid being followed, which meant not taking the usual paths.

Vaughn offered up his booted foot and she climbed on board. She'd found it simple to levitate through an unobstructed airspace, but she wasn't nearly so confident among all these trees.

Fergus shifted and flew like the wind on four paws, heading into the darkest part of the forest. Emma hugged Vaughn and kept her face buried against his shoulder. She wasn't used to watching trees flying at her. But she trusted Vaughn, who'd been levitating for eleven years, ever since he first became a vampire.

With so many twists, turns and double-backs through the pines, Emma had no idea which part of Savage she was in once they stopped moving. By the time she dove into the van alongside Vaughn, and the doors slammed shut, she happily accepted his strong arms once more. Savage roads sucked.

Do you think we eluded Loghry?

I have no idea, but Fergus did an outstanding job getting us to this point.

I'd have to agree.

The ride was bumpy through the territory. She knew exactly when the van reached Defiance Bridge, which led to Elegance, because suddenly they were rolling on smooth pavement. Defiance was one of the five large tri-part bridges that had given Five Bridges its name. The Savage Border Patrol worked their territory's end while the Elegance force checked vehicles and pedestrians at the entrance to spellcaster territory.

She was impressed that the van wasn't stopped at either checkpoints. Had to be Fergus's clout because they'd been waved through without incident at both ends of Defiance.

As another means of precaution, the driver of the van took a long, circuitous route getting to Emma's house. Even then, the driver stopped two streets north of her home to let them out.

The van took off immediately just as Vaughn covered them both with his vampire disguising shield. If there were warlocks or witches in the air, none of them would be able to see Vaughn and herself.

He flew her toward her home, and a split-second later they were descending into her backyard.

It was only two in the morning, and Emma had made it home alive.

Of course, the night wasn't over yet.

CHAPTER FIVE

I'd heard of the shifter fighting pits, but I'd never seen one before. The area it covered was smaller than I would have thought." Vaughn sat forward on a patio sofa, his gaze fixed to nothing in particular. He held the beer Emma had given him, dangling it between his knees with two fingers at the neck.

Her cat, Toby, would rub Vaughn's exposed and now-healed shin, then move to his jean-clad leg, weaving in his preferred figure-eight pattern. Vaughn would reach down once in a while and pet him.

Still standing, Emma leaned against the nearby Indian rosewood tree, but the rough-looking bark didn't seem to bother her back. She sipped a beer as well.

Divested of her Sig Sauer, her narrow waist was an invitation all over again. She'd released her long, auburn hair from the top knot, and it hung around her shoulders. She looked incredible.

"How's your leg?"

He glanced down. The wound had closed up completely, and he had no pain at all. "There's only some redness to show I'd gotten shot. Thanks for fixing me up."

She pushed away from the tree. "And thanks for helping me get those girls out."

He swigged his beer, finishing the rest. "Best feeling in the world." He set the bottle on the glass coffee table in front of him, settling it next to his Glock and holster. "They're probably home by now."

Emma moved near the sofa. "But will they stay there? Or will Loghry go after each and every one of them again?"

Vaughn flipped his hand back and forth, gesturing first to Stormy in the tree then the cat now half reclining on his left boot. "What do your friends say?"

Emma turned to the owl first, then glanced at Toby. Her quirky smile made another appearance. "They're still celebrating."

The owl lifted a clawed foot off the branch and hooted. The cat meowed in response. Vaughn was surprised, though he shouldn't have been. Emma was a powerful witch and some of that power had become part of her familiars. "I guess they are."

Emma moved closer and sat down, not exactly right next to him but not so far away he couldn't reach over and grab her. He worked hard to keep himself restrained, but he wanted her right now, something fierce.

She drank again and released a sigh. "How much of the ghosts can you see? And isn't it unusual for a vampire to see ghosts at all?"

"It is. As for what I can detect, at first, in the Graveyard, I didn't see anything. I only felt fingers on my face. Later, I had the impression of three faces, but right now," he paused and glanced at the figures sitting on top of a nearby dining table, "they're almost fully formed. They're even wearing clothes and seem to like the color red."

Emma chuckled. "That they do."

"Which one is Becca?"

"Our spokesperson ghost?" Emma shifted her gaze toward the table as well. "She's wearing the jeans and red tank top."

Vaughn stared at the triplets for a long time. They appeared to be communicating with each other. "The whole thing is amazing, that I can see them, that you can levitate and I can fly faster." He shifted toward her. "Speaking of that. How exactly did you discover you could levitate? It must have come as a big surprise."

She turned toward him as well, angling her body. "I've never been so shocked. But when we'd first arrived at the edge of forest and you moved me off your boot, I didn't touch the ground. I couldn't believe it. So while you were settling things with Fergus and his crew, I was gaining my bearings. The weirdest thing was having an absolute certainty that not only could I levitate, but I had the skills necessary to make it work. It was an incredible feeling."

"But how did this happen between us?" He turned more fully and planted his elbow on the back of the sofa. He rested his face against his fist. "I'm not getting what's going on here, why we seem to be sharing our different *alter* abilities."

She finished her beer and set the bottle next to his. She curled her knees up to better face him, then mirrored his movements by putting her elbow on the sofa as well. She rested her head against the palm of her hand. "Iris said the same kinds of things happened to her and Connor, a sort of sharing of gifts. Iris said she'd bit Seraphina and held her in a vampire thrall. That was one of the reasons they made their escape. Can you believe that?"

Vaughn leaned forward slightly. "I remember now. Connor said something about it, but it made no sense at the time. He said he could kill like a witch could. Jesus, this is a lot to take in." But there was something else he needed to talk over with her. "What the hell was all that about back there with Dagen-the-asshole? I was ready to kill him."

"I know. I could tell. And I really didn't want you in the pit with that monster. Once Max was out of the way, Dagen came after me. He wanted me to live with him as his mistress in Savage, since I could never be a real mate, at least in his eyes. Max had a different view entirely.

"I hate Dagen with a passion. There's something not right with him." Her nostrils flared. "He *smells* evil, the way the dark coven witches smell. It's hard to explain what that odor is like. It's as though some tinge of underworld sulphur catches hold of them. But if he really is mixed up with Loghry, then that would explain a lot."

"It would." He smiled suddenly. "I have to admit I loved it when you hit him."

"Oh, that's another thing. I mean, I lashed out because I was mad but I didn't expect to deliver a blow that could knock him off his feet. The thing is, the punch carried a portion of your strength. That's why he fell. This is just amazing and kind of hopeful. Maybe between us we have something that could battle a wizard of Loghry's ability. What do you think?"

Vaughn had only half listened to her words. He was caught up in his lust again, which increased because of the excited glitter in her eyes. The woman had a lot of life in her and he wanted some of that.

Using his free hand, he caressed Emma's face. "I think *you're* amazing. That's what I think. And thanks again for taking care of me in the field."

"It was my pleasure." Her cheeks took on a rosy hue.

His lips curved. "Now what are you thinking? Why are you blushing?"

She didn't answer him, instead, she moved very slowly, like a cat uncurling itself, and slid onto his lap. "This is why."

She kissed him, then nipped his lip. "I'm not proud of this, Vaughn, but part of me wanted you to take Dagen, to end up in the pit with him and tear him to shreds. When he was confronting me, I could feel your vampire power rise, and it was sexy as hell. The tension in your hand alone, because you were still holding mine right then, was a fire on my skin. I wanted you so much. And some of that desire is still with me."

He stared into her glinting green eyes, and his body responded instantly, which meant his jeans weren't fitting so well anymore. He would never know what she was like in her simple human form, but he loved her dynamic *alter* witch nature. She held nothing back, and this was something they shared in common. It was all or nothing.

She dipped down to suck on his neck, and that's when he felt it, a tenseness in her bite as though she had fangs. His mind loosened at the same time, a very strange sensation that he would describe as the beginnings of a vampire enthrallment.

He drew back and held her gaze. "Did you feel that, Em?"

"What? No. I don't know. I was just enjoying your throat."

"But that's my point. You were acting more like a vampire than a witch. You almost had me in a state of thrall."

"I did? Wait a minute, I did. You're right."

"Let me see your mouth. Bare your teeth for me."

She opened immediately for him. He rubbed along her gums

hunting for the swelling that would release a pair of fangs but nothing was there. When he started to remove his finger she caught it between her teeth, then drew it inside and sucked.

He groaned, and his jeans shrunk a little more. "I need out of these pants."

She let go of his finger. "And I need a shower, and I want you in it with me." In a swift levitating glide, she moved away from him, rising well above the coffee table. She didn't even hit the two beer bottles. She then pivoted midair as though she'd been flying all her life and sped to the glass doors that led into the house.

When the ghosts started to follow, she turned and wagged a finger at them. "Not allowed, girls. What's going to happen here is private."

All three looked downcast for a moment, then simply faded away.

Emma disappeared inside.

He followed in her wake, every cell of his body driven toward her. He felt consumed by his need. Once in the bathroom, he stripped quickly. She was already in the oversized shower, three heads flowing with water.

He had to laugh because she was spinning in a slow levitating move. It reminded him that he'd gone through his own aerial antics when he'd first become a vampire and realized he could fly.

When he joined her in the shower, she finally settled down and eased her feet to the tile floor. "You going to sex me up, Vaughn, or what?"

"Hell, yeah, I am."

~ ~ ~

As Vaughn reached for the bar of soap, Emma let her gaze move slowly over his massive shoulders. His arms were heavily muscled, and while he lathered up, she put her hands on his right arm and tried to span it with thumbs touching and pinky fingers as well. But couldn't.

"You're huge."

He glanced down at his cock then smiled wryly. "I am."

She chuckled. She liked Vaughn so much, even the way he joked with her. He planted his soapy hands on her breasts and began to massage.

She drew a deep breath and watched the intense expression on his face as he got busy.

He took his time feeling her up, smoothing his hands over her breasts and rubbing her sensitive nipples with his thumbs. She kept stroking his arms while he worked, loving how her hands rose and fell as she moved over his sculpted muscles.

She angled sideways, enough to get close to his left arm. He saw where she was headed so he released her nearest breast, which gave her just the right amount of room to kiss his bicep then open her mouth and sink her teeth. He pinched her nipple at the same time which had her moaning.

She pressed herself up against him and kept kissing, licking and biting his arm. His hand went to her bottom, squeezing her and holding her close so that she could feel he was completely erect.

He pushed the hair away from her neck and kissed her while she continued to nibble her way over all the different muscles. An image flashed in her mind of doing something similar, only with Vaughn flat on his back maybe even tied up at the wrists to keep him under control. The fantasy made her moan.

She moved up to his shoulder and continued her oral exploration. When he grabbed a good portion of her neck in his mouth, she grew very still. She loved the feel of it as though he was taking possession of her, staking his ownership. She felt a loose sensation move through her mind and knew she was partially enthralled, maybe because he hadn't bitten her.

She was at his command.

He slid his hand between her thighs, and his voice entered her mind. *Open for me.*

She took a side step, parting her legs for him. She moaned as his fingers drove inside and began working their own kind of magic. *Vaughn, I'm loving this.*

Me, too. I want to bite you. Would you like that, Emma? Would you like to feel my fangs?

A delicious shiver raced through her head to her toe. *Do it. Please. I need you drinking from me, with your fingers buried deep.*

He groaned as began licking her throat. He used a hand at the back of her neck to turn, then support her head.

The sting of his bite went straight to her sex, and as he began to take down her blood and slide his fingers in and out, a cry left her throat.

~ ~ ~

Vaughn drank greedily. Emma's blood tasted like a fine wine yet enhanced with the scent of her spellroom, very witchy, and he loved it. He thrust his fingers in and out of her body and he could tell by the way she kept crying out and the way her body writhed that he could make her come.

And he wanted the flavor of her orgasm in her blood.

He thrust his fingers faster. *Come for me, Emma. I want to feel your sex gripping my fingers and pulsing. Come for me, you beautiful witch. I love tapping into your vein. So much power.*

With that, he could feel her orgasm start to roll and wasn't surprised when she released a series of cries. He sustained the pace to keep the pleasure spiraling within her body.

When the cries stopped and her body grew lax, he slowed the drive of his wrist then finally withdrew his fingers from her body. He released her throat at the same time, swiping the wounds with his tongue to seal them.

He drew her against him, holding her tight. His eyes were closed as the water beat down on his back. Another spray hit Emma's shoulder.

He took deep breaths, savoring the feel of her blood working in his body. He felt as though small bits of electricity kept sizzling in his veins. He was pumped in the same way he'd been when she'd healed him. Something about Emma's power amplified his own and added to his skill set.

The power of her blood swirled through him and something more. His chest felt very full and warm, but it had nothing to do with his power or hers. Instead, he discovered a deep unsettling truth that somewhere in this nightmare he'd fallen in love with a witch.

But the next thought shredded him, that Five Bridges was no place to forge a relationship.

"That was fantastic, Vaughn."

He forced himself back to the present, and instead of pulling away, he caressed her back. "It was."

After a moment, he shifted so that he could meet her gaze. She looked satisfied and once more desire to be buried between her legs surged. He kissed her several times on the lips, one after the other, plucking and tasting.

Have you had fantasies about this, Vaughn?

Dozens, maybe hundreds. He could feel his eyelids grow heavy. *Some of them just like this, being in the shower with you and kissing you.*

This time, she drew back, caressing his face. "I've known love before, with Max. And I want you to know it's the same with you. I love you, Vaughn. I just never thought it would happen again and until tonight, I was afraid to put a name to what I was feeling. I wanted you to know, because the truth is neither of us knows what Loghry will do next."

For a moment, he froze. Would she expect him to tell her how he felt? He hoped not. He didn't want to speak the words aloud, to open that door, not when he was to blame for his sister's abduction.

Instead, he kissed her again, letting his body speak for how much she meant to him. Beyond that, he was unwilling to go. *How about we rinse off and test your bed to see how sturdy it is?*

Sounds perfect.

~ ~ ~

Emma's heart felt swollen in the best way. She hadn't been this content in a long time, not since Max. She wasn't surprised Vaughn hadn't responded to her expression of love by admitting to the same feelings. Something about the pressure of their immediate dire situation had made her bold. Beyond that, she had no expectations. She just wanted to be open and honest about what she was feeling for him.

She also knew that Vaughn carried a weight of guilt in his heart about losing his sister as he had. He'd never seen her again or discovered her body in a nightly check of the morgue, a ritual he'd undertaken for two years.

No, she had no expectations. This was Five Bridges, not the normal human world.

Vaughn carried her from the shower, dried her off, then levitated her to the bed. He continued to hold her in his arms as he pulled the comforter and pillows away.

The sheets were cool on her back as he laid her down. He climbed onto the bed to lie on his side next to her. She turned to face him.

He was so handsome with his dark gray eyes, straight black brows and strong, angled cheekbones.

He cupped her face and leaned close to kiss her. She parted her lips, and he drove inside, searching the depths of her mouth and making all kinds of promises. As he shifted to move over her chest, she was able to caress his arms again, then his back. She wiggled closer to feel his thighs against hers. She pushed his hip and he drew back enough for her to stroke his cock with her hand.

Vaughn?

Yes?

His tongue teased the depths of her mouth. She forgot for a moment what she was going to ask him.

When she remembered, she leaned away just a little and thumbed his lips. "I'm really hungry."

"You are? You mean you want something to eat?" He looked concerned and started to get up.

She caught his elbow, pulling him back down, then pushing him onto his back. "I wanted you to feed me. That's all. Then maybe you'll get hungry and want something to eat as well." She was being bold, but how much time would they really have together after this night?

He groaned and spread his legs as she moved between his thighs. His cock stood upright, and when he leaned up and cupped the back of her neck, she slowly lowered her mouth to him. She held his gaze as she licked the tip.

His lips trembled, and his cock jerked.

With one hand, she held him firmly at the base, then surrounded the crown with her mouth. She didn't suck right away. Instead she swirled her tongue over the head, teasing the rim the entire distance.

His hips rocked, and he moaned. With his hand still on the back of her neck, he squeezed gently, pushing at the same time. She got the message.

She took him deeper in her mouth and finally made the first sucking motion. An odd sound came out of his mouth, sort of an anguished grunt. Once more, she sucked, only this time drawing slowly up at the same time, then pushing back down with her lips and mouth.

"You need to stop."

She released him. "So soon?" she smiled. "But I was just getting started."

"I don't want to come yet. I want to make this last."

"How about I ride you, then?"

His sudden smile looked devilish. "You forget. I'm hungry, too."

Another shiver raced through her.

He beckoned her forward with a crook of his index finger. "I'm thinking you should bring your hips close to my mouth, then hold onto the headboard with both hands."

Her turn to make an odd sound, only hers was part squeak, part moan. She carefully moved up his body, balancing herself with a hand on either side of him. When she had her knees beside his head, he grabbed her hips and pulled her sex down to him. She moaned as he licked a long line up her clitoris.

The pleasure was so intense that she cried out. She also gripped the headboard, just as he'd ordered. Using his hands, he tilted her hips at a strong angle. She moaned again, knowing what he meant to do. She gasped as his tongue found her entrance.

He guided her with his hands on her hips and buttocks and created a steady pumping motion. He was damn strong and used all that power now to work her deep inside.

He flicked his tongue fast, then swirled. He was a big man and even his tongue filled her.

He kept moving faster and plunging her hips up and down at the same time. She'd never been tongue-fucked like this before, and it was more erotic than anything she'd ever experienced.

She groaned and cried out.

Come for me again, Emma. I love how your orgasm flavors your blood, and I plan to bite you again. Come for me. Come now!

Suddenly, the orgasm was right there. He must have known because he moved his tongue vampire fast and she came almost shouting. And what was that sensation? Like small, pleasurable shocks of electricity that had her hips jumping.

The pleasure intensified and moved in rapid pulses up through her abdomen. She cried out repeatedly.

When the wave finally passed, her body turned to jelly. She slid off to the side of Vaughn and rolled onto her back. "What did you do? That was amazing. I swear I felt a kind of electricity the whole time."

He rolled once more onto his side and gently rubbed her abdomen. "I thought it was coming from you. But whatever this is, it has me hard as a rock."

"Maybe it's us, how we are together."

"I don't know. This whole night has been full of surprises." He drew close and kissed her abdomen and even tongued her navel.

She ran her hand through his thick top hair, pushing it back, then raking her nails over the nearly bald tattooed area. "I love these tattoos on the side of your head. All the sword-like points are very sexy."

He kissed his way down her abdomen and placed several on her sex. "I could spend another hour just tasting you over and over."

Emma drew in a deep breath and squeezed her eyes shut, because suddenly her chest hurt. She wanted him to spend hours, then days, then years doing to her whatever he wanted.

But the reality of their situation and that Loghry had known they would be at the storage facility swept over her like a terrible storm. Tears flowed so fast she couldn't stop them.

"Hey, what's wrong?"

She opened her eyes and saw that he was now on his hands and knees. He stroked her cheeks, swiping at the tears. "Why are you crying?"

"I don't want this to end. I want years with you, Vaughn. Dammit, I want decades."

He kissed her suddenly. Had she seen tears in his eyes as well?

~ ~ ~

Vaughn's eyes burned. He couldn't remember the last time he'd felt this way. He was in bed with a woman, and a witch at that, but he wanted years as well, not just this one damn night.

When she grabbed his arm and pulled him toward her, he took the hint. He moved his knees between her legs.

"You said you'd bite me again, and I really want you to."

He nodded, searching her face. She caressed his neck, his shoulders, his arms. He took his cock in hand and pressed it against her well and began to push.

Her body did a rolling wave, the pleasure between them very mutual. The same small jolts of electricity jumped between them, adding another sensual layer.

He took his time entering her. Between thrusts, he kissed her forehead, her cheeks, her throat. She settled her hands on his pecs and fondled him, teasing his nipples.

When he was deep inside, he set a slow rhythm, wanting to savor every moment, knowing it could be their last time together. He planted his forearms on either side of her so he could make as much body-contact as possible. She wrapped her arms around him and he kissed her hard, driving his tongue deep.

She responded with a mournful cry against his mouth. He knew she was overcome.

He was, too.

He kissed his way down her cheek and along her neck, hunting for the right spot. But this time, piercing her vein felt like so much more than a feeding. It was an intimate connection he needed to make with her.

She turned her head. "Yes, Vaughn. I want this more than anything. I want to feel your thrall."

Her fingers sizzled with power, an erotic sensation wherever she touched him. He knew in a concentrated dose, the same energy could kill him. Yet he loved what she was doing, because it came from her, from who she was as a powerful *alter* witch.

He licked her throat above the vein. She was breathing hard, waiting.

He paused in his thrusts, drew his head back, then struck with his fangs to the right depth. Her blood flowed into his mouth once more, and he groaned. The flavor was full of her ecstasy, and he trembled as it went down his throat. Once it hit his stomach, power and desire exploded together.

He arched his hips and began to drive into her forcefully, deep thrusts the length of her sex. He loved being buried between her legs and hearing her moans. She tilted her pelvis, catching and squeezing his cock.

He shook now from the power he was feeling and the need to fill her full of what he had to give as a man.

In this moment, she was his woman.

His woman.

You're mine, Emma. All mine.

I belong to you, Vaughn, no matter how much time we have together. I'm yours fully and completely, nothing held back. The sensation of thrall is incredibly erotic. I love being captured by you in this way, held so that I can't move except to respond to your body.

He groaned at her words and moved faster. She uttered a series of cries as she wrapped her legs around his waist.

He released her throat, swiping the wounds to close them off, then lifted up so he could look down at her. She was panting, on the edge. She was so beautiful, her lips swollen and her eyes dilated with pleasure and desire.

"Fuck me, Vaughn. Fuck me hard."

He groaned at her words, then increased the pace, moving as fast as he could.

She opened her mouth, arched her neck and began to cry out, a wild sound that took him the rest of the way.

His balls tightened. "I'm coming." He released into her and pleasure filled his head with a mighty wind. The electricity from her hands became an electrical field that took his pleasure and spread it all over his body.

He shouted first, then roared, a sound matched only by her cries of ecstasy.

After a moment, he began to ease back, but he felt it again, that he'd be releasing a second time. "Emma, do you want more?"

Her body writhed beneath his. "Yes. Fill me again."

He nodded as the need to ejaculate gripped his groin. Once more, he quickened his pace. She moved her hands over his back and the electricity began to work on him again.

He grunted as he pushed. Then suddenly it was there, the release that had him moving faster and his hips jerking. She dug her nails into his back, which somehow sent the electricity into his bones, and it felt incredibly erotic.

The pleasure was profoundly intense, and he was roaring once more, joining her cries.

When he was finally empty, he began to slow, then stop.

Emma's body fell lax at almost the same moment. She spread her arms wide on the bed, her eyes closed, breathing hard through her mouth.

He was in a similar state, all but panting. He eased down to rest his massive body on hers, though supporting some of his weight with his forearms.

His back still hummed where she'd sent her strange witchy energy, and it calmed him as nothing else had in his entire *alter* existence.

~ ~ ~

Emma had never been as content as she was right now with Vaughn's weight on her and his cock still inside her. She loved him and for this moment in time, they were one.

Dawn was a couple of hours away yet. Her security spell held. She would keep Vaughn safe in her home through the day.

Though her arms were limp, she forced herself to surround him and hug him. "Thank you, Vaughn. That was so magical. Unbelievable."

He lifted up enough to look at her. "Your hands created the most amazing kind of energy over my skin and more pleasure than I've ever known."

She leaned up and kissed him, then lowered her head to the pillow. "I'm so glad. And I love that you're still connected to me. Will you stay the night, or rather the day?"

He nodded. "Of course I will. More than anything I want this time with you, no matter what the future holds."

She smiled. "Do you know what I want right now?"

"What's that?"

"A meal, then a bath with you in it. How does that sound?"

"I'm not much of a tub man, but if you're in it, believe me, I'm game. And I wouldn't say no to some food."

She caught his face with her hands. "Then we'll have this time together, these few hours, maybe the day as well?"

He kissed her. "Yes. We'll have that."

~ ~ ~

Vaughn shared a bath with Emma, then made love to her repeatedly until they both lay exhausted on her bed and fell sound asleep. More than once he woke up because she was thrashing in her sleep. He suspected nightmares and took her in his arms each time, holding her close until she settled down.

And each time, his heart bound itself to her a little more until he wasn't sure he was even a separate entity. When he finally woke for the night, and the last rays of the sun were heading west, Emma was still asleep, her body pressed up against his.

He had his arm around her and stared up at the central overhead fan. The blades looked special-made and had unique carvings. Maybe she spent time staring at them.

Now he was.

He didn't want the night to begin. He wanted to stay here forever.

Emma began to stir, then stretch as she rolled onto her back. But she stayed reclining on his arm and eventually took his hand in hers and squeezed his fingers.

She seemed tense and no wonder given the number of times she'd tossed and turned. "Emma, did you have bad dreams last night?"

She was silent for a moment. "Yeah, I did. How did you know?"

He told her about how restless she'd been.

"That bad, huh?"

"Yes. Want to talk about it?"

She sighed heavily. "I dreamed about Loghry, though I really don't know why. He's so strange looking. He's emaciated as addicts often are and his skin is paper white. And his lips have a violet color.

"But each time he appeared, I had this creepy feeling he was really seeing me in my dreams, sort of like a fae who can dreamscape. That's what distressed me so much.

"In one of the dreams, I was running through a dark maze with Loghry chasing me. I just couldn't find my way out."

When she shuddered, he pulled her close. "I'm sorry you had such a bad night."

"It's okay. I'll get over it." She sighed once more. "Did you ever meet Loghry?"

"Once, years ago. Though he didn't look quite so bad as you've just described. I don't think he'd been in Five Bridges for very long, but he'd already taken up the dark arts.

"Several Crescent officers, including myself, were called to the scene. We found him strangling a female vampire, who had just expired. He was strung out on amethyst flame, no doubt about that. And powerful as hell because of the drug.

"We beat him to get him off the woman, then he turned his wizard powers on us. I got a couple of rounds off and I know at least one of the bullets struck home. One of the men used his sword as well, cutting him deep in his abdomen.

"After several minutes, he finally fell down dead. Or at least that's what we thought. We even hauled him off to the morgue."

She lifted up on her elbow. "Wait, I remember this. He came back to life and walked out, didn't he?"

"That's exactly what happened. There was no one watching at the morgue, so it wasn't hard for him to just pick up and go."

She flopped back down, her head resting on his shoulder. "That bastard needs to die for good."

"Yes, he does."

His gaze once more went to the fan. Maybe a change of subject was in order. He gestured toward the ceiling with his free arm. "The carving on the wood is beautiful."

"It was a gift from Max."

Vaughn repressed a sigh. Right now he was jealous of Max, for all the time he'd had with Emma. "Sounds like he was a good man."

She rolled to look up at him, her hand on his chest. "He was. I think you would have been good friends if you'd known each other. He was an excellent Savage Border Patrol officer and a great alpha to his pack."

He reached toward her and pushed her hair behind her ear. "We probably would have been friends. He sounds like he was in Fergus's mold, someone I respect."

"Yeah, very much like Fergus."

"So, one question, Trib officer. How the hell can you look so beautiful first thing at night?"

She laughed. "I'm sure I don't. You need glasses, my friend."

"We're *alters*. We don't do glasses."

She chuckled again. "Now I have a question for you. I'm thinking about fixing an omelet with mozzarella, tomatoes and basil. Maybe some toast and coffee. How does that sound?"

He rubbed his growling stomach. "Sold."

She laughed again as she left the bed and headed into the bathroom. "Shower, first."

He could have joined her, and even thought about it for a good long minute. But that would have led to other things and his instincts told him he needed to turn his attention to the night.

He and Emma had gotten lucky so far. They'd lived through last night and today, yet nothing had substantially changed. Loghry would still be after them. Better to face the madman right away than waste some serious hunting time by bringing Emma back to bed.

And there was the heart of the difficulty. He'd want to stay put for hours, not just enjoy a quickie.

He rolled from bed and crossed to the French doors. Pushing them open, he looked up into the graying sky. He could see a few stars already. Full dark was only a half hour away.

He had to avoid looking directly at the distant western horizon. The vampire *alter* serum had followed mythical protocol to the letter; vampires were seriously sun allergic. He'd blistered up once or twice in the early days when, without thinking, he'd stepped into direct sunlight. The pain had been unbearable, the light not just burning the surface skin, but somehow sinking deep and cutting into the bones.

But the arrival of dusk created another reason he stayed the course and left Emma alone. As a Crescent Border Patrol officer, his senses lit up the moment the sun dropped beyond the horizon. The criminal insanity of Five Bridges at night called to his need for order and justice. Maybe it was his training and years of service, but right now his attention was fixed on Loghry and devising a reasonable strategy for attacking the man where he lived.

~ ~ ~

Emma was grateful Vaughn didn't follow her to the shower, though she would have welcomed him all the same. She had a job to do and felt its critical nature deep in her witchy bones.

She needed her coffee and her omelet, then some time in meditation to try to figure out what she and Vaughn should do next.

As she dried her hair, what weighed on her mind was how Loghry had known she and Vaughn would be at the storage facility. She recalled how the series of snapshot images had become scrambled suddenly. Was it possible Loghry had interfered with her meditation?

Movement caught her eye. Vaughn appeared at the bathroom entrance, then strolled in. For a moment, all her resolution faltered since he was buck naked. He looked as gorgeous as ever, though his straight black brows were pulled together in a tight line of concentration. "Don't worry, I'm just here for a shower."

He came up behind her, however, and slid his arms around her in a gentle embrace. He met her gaze in the mirror. "But I almost ran after you when you left the bed. Thought you should know."

She sighed. "Wish we could just go back there."

"I know. I've been torn as well, but getting Loghry before he gets us has consumed my thoughts." He leaned down, pushed her hair away and kissed her neck. "I love you, Emma."

She gasped softly. "You do?"

"I didn't say it last night, but I should have, so I'm saying it now. I fell hard for you the night we saved those girls. I can admit it now. Just wish everything was different."

"Me, too."

He didn't look at her again as he moved in the direction of the shower.

She let him go, though she was overcome that he'd said he loved her. She had a strong suspicion that if he didn't believe their nights were numbered, he would never have said the words out loud. She knew Vaughn. She knew what the loss of his sister had done to him, and that even if they somehow survived an encounter with Loghry, he wouldn't be able to handle a long-term relationship with her.

She wasn't much different. Max's death had ruined something inside her as well. She doubted she would have said anything either, if their situation hadn't been so dire.

But it was and in the same way Vaughn was focused on Loghry, her thoughts were fixed on her spellroom. She also knew the triplets were inside waiting for her. Time to get on with things, and they both needed a good meal.

A few minutes later, she had the front half of her hair in a top knot, then crossed to the dressing room to get ready. She wore her jeans and sturdy leather belt, socks and running shoes, and the short-sleeved t-shirt all the female Trib officers wore, lavender this time.

She picked up her holster, then left the bedroom.

Her kitchen was one of her favorite places to be, something that had very little to do with her witchness. The part of her still very human loved to cook.

She ground her coffee beans fresh, then finished the process with her French press. While her coffee steeped, she went to her herb garden and collected a few sprigs of fresh basil. The scent always got to her, easing her mind. The flavor was exactly what she wanted with her eggs, cheese and tomatoes.

She crossed paths with Vaughn on her way back, who had a cup of coffee in hand. He was dressed in one of Max's long navy t-shirts as well as a fresh pair of jeans. He'd cleaned up his tough, black leather work-boots and looked fantastic.

"Enjoy the garden."

"I will."

She stopped long enough to take hold of his arm, rise up on tiptoes and kiss him. Then she headed to finish up her kitchen duties.

As she moved in the direction of the house, she didn't have to look back to know he was watching her. If either of them made enough of a push, they'd be locked together once more.

But she could sense his determination probably because it matched her own.

"Breakfast in ten."

"Thanks," he called back.

She served the meal on the back patio behind her spellroom. The early April weather was almost balmy in the evenings. She'd flung the doors wide so she could begin connecting with the space long before she entered her meditation.

Vaughn didn't say a word as he sat down and began to eat. His gaze rarely landed on her, but she could feel him thinking. She doubted he tasted one bite of his food.

"Loghry?"

He glanced at her and nodded. "Yep."

"Same here."

She felt in her bones they'd be facing the psychopathic wizard before the night was out.

CHAPTER SIX

Vaughn ate methodically, but his thoughts were consumed with Loghry and trying to put a strategy together.

More often than not, his gaze landed inside the spellroom. He didn't know why Emma had purposely opened the doors, but he suspected it had something to do with her connection to the space. He was hoping she'd revisit her snapshot images again, the same process that had led them to rescue the girls in Savage.

If she could get a vision involving Loghry's mansion, they'd have a chance of taking the wizard on. More than anything, he wanted to end Loghry's reign of terror against young teenage girls.

"You squeeze that fork any harder, you'll bend it in half."

Frowning, Vaughn glanced at Emma. "What?"

"Your fork." She gestured to his hand. "Will I have to replace it?"

He glanced down and saw that he'd compressed it, bending the tines almost to the tip of the handle. "Shit. I'm sorry, Em."

"Something particular on your mind?" She slipped a bite of omelet into her mouth

"Loghry and his victims. I'm hoping you can bring up a new set of snapshots tonight. I'm jumping to get a chance at Loghry. Or if not him, then to rescue some more girls." He picked up his mug and drank. The coffee had cooled, but he didn't care.

"I was thinking I could try focusing on Loghry's mansion."

He smiled. "You read my mind."

"Not hard to do since we both want the same thing."

He took her hand and gave it a squeeze. "We do."

He appreciated Emma and approved of her drive. However, he didn't like the idea of her anywhere near Loghry. He kept trying to arrange scenarios in his head that would keep her safe.

He watched her eat, then unbent his fork and went to work on his meal as well. He had no idea what they'd be facing, but food was as much a necessity for a vampire warrior as blood.

~ ~ ~

As soon as Emma had the dishes cleaned up, she headed to her spellroom.

Vaughn came with her, but the moment she reached the threshold, she stopped.

"What's wrong?"

"I'm nervous. I know once I go in, everything will change." Her throat closed up tight, as she turned toward him. "I mean, we may not make it back here alive."

He surrounded her with his arms and pulled her close. "Maybe I should go alone. Or I could give Brannick a call. I have a number of friends on the Crescent Border Patrol who would throw in without a second's thought. Hell, I could call Fergus. He'd be happy to bring his crew into Elegance and help take this bastard down."

Emma wrapped her arms around Vaughn's waist, but she shook her head. "There's a big part of me that wants you to do exactly that. But you and I are a team now, that's what I know to be true. We do this together."

He drew back. "Emma, let me do this for you. I have resources with Crescent that you don't have with the Trib. This could work and dammit, I want you safe. You've done enough."

Every instinct Emma possessed told her going after Loghry was her fate as well, that she needed to be there. But she could see from the determined light in Vaughn's eye that he was warming quickly to the idea of leaving her behind.

Knowing the male warrior mind as she did, she chose the diplomatic course. "Let me prepare a new spell and settle into my meditation. I won't make any decision without being connected to my witch abilities. Then, if it's clear your course is the one we ought to take, I won't argue. How does that sound?"

He smiled wryly. "It's not exactly what I wanted to hear, but I agree that your witch ability should be involved, especially because we're dealing with a wizard."

~ ~ ~

Vaughn followed Emma into the spellroom, and immediately his mind grew clouded with the level of power in the space. He had to pause for a moment to gain his bearings. The owl was on his perch facing the door to the backyard, but he swung his head around to have a good look at Vaughn.

When Vaughn acclimated to the room, he remained at a distance. He felt irritable as he watched Emma begin her preparations. The warrior in him needed to get going, to start making a plan to catch Loghry in his home. He also didn't want Emma in danger. If there was a way he could prevent her from going, he'd do it.

She ground herbs, seeds and twigs with a mortar and pestle, the various scents filling the air. The whole time her power rolled at him in waves. His mind grew loose again, yet the muscles of his body twitched with readiness. It was a strange combination of sensations.

She drank her potion, then carried the small, red ceramic bowl from her worktable to the *chaise-longue* and slid it beneath. She took her time lighting the previous arc of seven candles above the area where she would settle her head.

When she lay down, he felt disconnected from her, maybe because he'd lost his motivation to have her with him when he went to Loghry's.

~ ~ ~

Emma knew this experience was completely different from the last one with Vaughn. He was keeping his distance but not for a selfish reason. His desire to keep her safe was why he wanted to go it alone and it warmed her heart to know he cared so much.

However, protection wasn't what she needed right now. She had her own score to settle with the vile wizard who had tormented so many girls all these years. She could only hope that somewhere in the process of reaching into the future, Vaughn would accept whatever role she was supposed to play.

The triplets arrived but they were in a solemn state. Becca didn't attempt to communicate telepathically. Instead, she waited with her sisters and offered one serious dip of her chin. Clearly, the ghosts believed she was on the right path.

She drew a deep breath, the nature of her witchy power stronger than ever. She kept herself open to what the future might tell her. After all, it was possible she and Vaughn were meant to go somewhere else besides Loghry's home. Therefore, she didn't focus on anything specific at first, but let her mind move from her spellroom all the way to Savage Territory and even over to Crescent.

But only as she dwelled on Elegance did a few snapshots finally emerge. The moment she settled on Loghry's mansion, sure enough, the images increased and formed a spinning carousel in her mind.

Her heartrate ramped up. Tonight would be about the wizard.

His mansion was only three miles away near one of the few hills in the Elegance portion of Phoenix. Within the connected snapshots, she saw herself flying beside Vaughn, which settled the matter of her going once and for all.

They would do this together. Vaughn would simply have to adjust to her role in the night's events.

The images moved rapidly, so she engaged as she had last time, placing herself within the stream of snapshots. She flew over the top of the mansion all the way past the pool and landed behind a distant guest house. Trees cloaked the area, which made it an excellent location for entering Loghry's several-acre complex.

Once on the ground, she and Vaughn passed through a gate, then descended a set of stone steps leading below the guest house and well into the earth.

She knew then that she'd located Loghry's infamous labyrinth, the place he supposedly kept a female vampire locked up. Rumors had it she suffered from a second-hand addiction to amethyst flame because of the wizard's lust for the powerful flame drug combined with his need to have a vampire drinking from him.

Within the images, she followed Vaughn, levitating behind him through a series of pillars and narrow stone passageways. Electric light bulbs, encased in small wire cages, hung from posts at various intervals but were never bright enough to fully illuminate any given space. She could feel the sinister nature of the structure, how the maze-like web of paths would make it difficult for anyone to escape.

She heard the sound of distant weeping and watched Vaughn turn to the right to follow the curve of the strange underground space. She felt herself directing him to make a series of turns, one after the other, as though she'd always known how to navigate the labyrinth.

The last path led them to the heart of the maze with a huge open area of dirt surrounded by a dozen large cages. All of them were empty except two. The biggest cage, directly across from Emma, held five human female teens. Three of them were weeping. Each was badly bruised.

A hissing sound drew Emma's attention to the other occupied cage at her right.

The space was like a jail cell because it had a toilet, a sink and a cot, but nothing else. The floor, like the rest of the central part of the labyrinth, was made of dirt.

The woman inside, a vampire, wore a dirty, red tunic and crouched on all fours as though ready to spring. She had mottled violet flame marks on her arms, neck and face, indicating she satisfied her blood needs from a donor addicted to amethyst flame. The mottling was a sure sign of second-hand addiction.

So here she was, the fabled woman Loghry had kept imprisoned in his labyrinth for years.

The woman, her black hair hanging over her face, leaped at the bars, latching on with her hands and toes like a wild animal. "He's coming for you. Don't you see? He's created this vision to draw you here, then he'll kill you."

Emma was so startled by her vehemence and by the wild light in her gray eyes that the images scattered like leaves caught by a sudden wind.

She blinked and opened her eyes.

Vaughn still stood far away, near Stormy's post. The owl blinked his large eyes at her.

Emma sat up and met Vaughn's gaze. "We were in Loghry's labyrinth, together, you and I. We made it to the center, but there were five more girls caged there who need to be rescued. I saw a deranged female vampire as well, locked up in a cage. Vaughn, this isn't about Loghry tonight. It's about saving these girls."

She then shared all the details of the vision.

~ ~ ~

Vaughn didn't know what to think. He'd been prepared to tell Emma he couldn't let her go into another dangerous situation. She served as a Trib officer and rarely saw the kind of action the Border Patrol officers encountered.

But it appeared the nature of the mission had gotten changed up to a rescue operation.

Emma rose from her couch and drew close to him. "Vaughn, what's going on here? You had no problem with me going into Savage. How is this different?"

He settled his hands on her arms. Jesus his throat was tight. "I don't want you to get hurt."

She nodded. "I know. I get it. I don't want you to get hurt either."

"What if it's a trap?"

She shrugged but planted her hands on his chest, her strange witchy electricity flowing over him. "I'm pretty confident that's exactly what it is. But we were there, you and I, together. Neither of us held back. I won't say I'm not scared, because I am. But we have to do this, both of us."

Vaughn released a heavy sigh. "I've been trying to avoid this moment ever since I took you to bed. I don't want this time with you to end and I don't want you to get hurt. I know you should go. My instincts confirm that you need to do this. But I hate it."

She slid her hands up to caress his shoulders. "If it helps, I don't want to go either. I'd rather stay here with you secure in my home until the end of time. But we're beyond all that, aren't we? I mean, we live and work and battle impossible enemies because we're both *alter* creatures and we live in this hellhole."

He pulled her tight against him. "Being with you felt so normal. That's all. And I wanted more of it, greedy bastard that I am."

She drew back, smiling up at him. "I'd almost join a dark coven if it meant I'd get to spend one more night with you."

At that, he smiled. "No you wouldn't." He stroked a hand the length of her hair.

"I said 'almost'. But you're right. I'd die before I took up the dark arts."

"And that's exactly why I don't want my time with you to end. I love who you are in this world. You've been the biggest surprise and you've given me something I shouldn't be feeling. Something like hope."

"I know what you mean. After Max died, I shut down. I wasn't willing to go through that kind of pain again. Then we pulled the triplets out of Loghry's flower van and it changed things for me."

He nodded slowly. "It did, including what we both need to do next."

"And that we need to do it together."

"Yes. Together." He was resigned now. He knew this was the right thing. "So, tell me everything you saw in this recent vision so we can start planning."

She reviewed the details once more up to the point the female vampire frightened her and the images scrambled.

"And it was just you and me?"

"Yes. I didn't see anyone else around. No one."

"And no guards at the gate? Or on the property?" It sounded suspicious to him.

"No guards. Nothing."

"And above the property, you didn't see an active spell? Anything that might prevent us from flying to this central area?"

She shook her head in response. "You also have to remember that

Wizard Loghry is one of the most powerful warlocks in Elegance. I might not even be able to detect a spell he created. On the other hand, he may believe his reputation is strong enough to keep his enemies away. "

"And no obvious signs of a security system?" Vaughn had always heard that Loghry's mansion had a high-tech set-up. He said as much to Emma.

She shrugged. "I don't know what to tell you. I encountered nothing like that. Which of course makes it all sound like a trap."

"Yes, it does."

"Do you think we should try a different approach?"

"I think we need back-up. It's clear from your vision that we'll make it inside, but who knows what we'll face coming out. I'm going to call Brannick and Fergus. I have no doubt they'll want in on this."

Emma leaned up and kissed him. Familiar erotic jolts of electricity moved over his lips, reminding him of everything they'd done in bed together, all the hours spent tangled up and lost in each other's arms.

He returned the kiss, feeling desperate. He drew back, but not to let her go. Instead, he pulled her into a tight embrace and held on.

When at last he released her, Emma took a deep breath. "I think calling the troops is exactly what we should do. And if we stick together, we might be able to get these girls out."

He nodded. "I'll make some calls."

~ ~ ~

When Vaughn left the spellroom, Emma headed back to her bedroom. The labyrinth was cold, so she made the decision to switch out her short-sleeved t-shirt for one with long sleeves, tucking it in so she would still have access to her gun. She threaded her belt through the pant loops.

She brushed out her hair again, more to calm her nerves than anything else. Securing the top knot, she pushed the rest past her shoulders to lie in a wave down her back. She turned while looking at herself in the mirror. Her hair was almost to her waist.

Her cheeks grew flushed as she recalled a time in bed early this morning, when Vaughn, while taking her from behind, kept kissing and petting her hair. It had been very tender, yet erotic.

She didn't want this time with Vaughn to end and for a few seconds hot tears brimmed in her eyes.

Giving herself a shake, she returned to her bedroom and clipped her holster onto her belt and checked her Sig. She'd been unable to see what happened after they reached the center of the underground labyrinth, but Loghry was a wizard of great power. It might be a simple thing to get in, but a very different matter trying to leave.

Once she was dressed, she met Vaughn outside. He wore his Glock and holster and was full of tension. The triplets hovered nearby, but were as grim-faced as before, another sure sign how important the mission was.

Becca? Everything okay?

She nodded. *Going to Loghry's will be very dangerous. We're worried for you guys.*

You don't have to come with.

Becca glanced at each of her sisters in turn. *We want to. This is the man who stole our lives and if we can help to bring him down, even in a small way, we want to do that.*

Okay, then.

When she reverted her attention to Vaughn, she saw he was watching the girls. His gaze slipped back to her. "What did they say?"

"They're worried about the mission, but they'll be with us and will do what they can."

His straight black brows were drawn tightly together. "All right. Sounds good." He nodded several times as though regrouping his thoughts. "Brannick will be in the air above your house soon. He's bringing my half-sword because we don't know what we're going to find once we're inside. He's in the process of coordinating back-up. He's contacted a couple of trustworthy Elegance Border Patrol officers and Fergus in Savage wanted in on anything have to do with shutting Loghry down. We'll have a mixed-force detail."

She nodded. "I think this is fantastic." Until last night, she'd thought she was alone in her battle against the perverse, brutal elements of Five Bridges.

He gripped her arms. "Are you ready for this, Em, for whatever we find?"

"I am."

A smile touched his lips as he released her arms then glanced down at her feet. "Let me see you levitate."

He probably thought she'd lift up a couple of inches. Instead, she shot into the air then came down behind him and jumped on his back.

He caught her legs so that she was essentially having a piggy-back ride. She surrounded his neck with both arms, then leaned into him and kissed his cheek. "I love you, Vaughn. Whatever happens, I love you."

He caught her arms with both hands and squeezed. "Back atcha."

When his cell made a soft ding, he pulled it from the pocket of his jeans while keeping her balanced on his back. He spoke quietly for a couple of minutes, then put it away. "Brannick's not far, just east of your house. He said the skies are clear and he has my weapons. We're ready to go."

"Then let's go."

She eased off his back, but didn't land on the ground. Instead, she flew straight up, moving through her security spell and into the sky. He joined her. The ghosts traveled near Emma, but were still somber and very quiet.

Sure enough, Brannick and five other Crescent officers were hovering above a house on the next street over from Emma's.

Once she and Vaughn reached them, Brannick handed Vaughn his sword. Vaughn, wearing one of Max's belts, clipped on the sword sheath and re-checked his Glock.

She could feel Vaughn communicating with Brannick telepathically. The entire team was tense but remained silent, each officer repeatedly checking the skies from all directions.

Emma did as well. But Brannick was right. There were no Elegance warlocks or witches out tonight, at least not right now, which matched the images in her vision.

When Brannick and his men took off west to meet up with Fergus and his squad, Vaughn met Emma's gaze. *Shall we get this party started?*

With pleasure.

As she flew in the direction of Loghry's mansion, she reached for Vaughn's hand. He grabbed it and gave her fingers a squeeze, then released it.

She didn't say the words out loud, but she didn't need to. They both knew there was a good chance tonight neither of them would make it out of the labyrinth alive.

~ ~ ~

Vaughn had never been this torn in his entire life. He wanted Emma with him. But at the same time he wished she was heading anywhere other than Loghry's fortress-like residence, complete with a labyrinth dungeon.

He forced himself to remember that she wasn't just a woman he loved, but she was a trained Tribunal officer and knew how to use her weapon. She might not have had as much experience as he did in actual shoot-outs, but she had grit.

Her voice entered his mind. *We're exactly where we're supposed to be according to the vision.*

Good. What else could he say? He wanted to turn around, take her back to her house, and chain her up so she'd be safe. But that door was now shut tight.

As he flew directly over the mansion, he saw no sign of Brannick which was a good thing. The support team would come in from the opposite end of the property and hide in the trees to wait for the rescue. If Emma had seen any of them in the underground maze, he would have asked them to join their below-ground mission in a heartbeat.

He followed Emma's lead and headed toward the guest house, well beyond the pool. Once there, he dropped down behind what was a small stone structure, an unusual choice for the desert. The gate was right where she'd said it would be. She reached for the latch, but he wasn't willing to let her go first, no matter how much courage she had.

He caught her arm and held her gaze, though he spoke telepathically. *I don't care what your vision showed you, I'm going in first.*

But her quirky smile appeared. *Oh, don't worry. You went before me. And believe me, I won't argue with you on this one.*

He couldn't help but smile. She knew the chances they were taking, but she could still joke with him. Yeah, the woman had grit.

He drew his sword from its sheath, then his Glock. He wanted both weapons in hand.

Were we running or levitating?

Levitating, to keep the noise level down.

Got it. He moved slowly, floating just above the stone steps. When he got to the bottom, the entrance led to the right. He grabbed the knob and turned, then pushed. The damn door wasn't even locked, another sign they were being drawn into Loghry's lair. Bastard.

He saw the small caged lights, just as Emma had described them, as well as the stone walls and deep shadows. The smell was musty, but not surprising.

At the outset, three paths presented themselves. *Which way?*

Take the center path, then the one that bends slightly to the left.

He moved swiftly and she continued to give him directions. *Make a quick right, left, then right again. Yes, this is it. Now take the straight path, but it will veer to the left.*

He heard the girls weeping, just as Emma had said they would be. He could feel her flying behind him, sticking close.

When he reached another branch of three, her voice hit his mind. *We're almost there. Turn right, but swing back left, then we should be in the center.*

He sped quickly, slowing only to make sure that when he took a turn, he didn't collide with anything unexpected. But the path was unobstructed and opened almost immediately to the wrought iron cages Emma had described.

Opposite, he saw the five girls clumped together, comforting each other. *Were they huddled like this in the vision?*

Yes.

And I see that the triplets are floating near them. What are they doing?

I think they're trying to comfort the girls. If anyone knows how they would be feeling right now, Becca and her sisters would.

No doubt about that.

A hiss behind Vaughn had him turning to face the female vampire, the only other prisoner present. So, the rumors were true that Loghry kept a woman locked up to feed from him.

She looked like an animal. Her bare feet hugged a lower section of the cell-like bars while her hands grabbed at an upper part. Violet-colored flames, though mottled, streaked over the bared portion of her chest and throat and up the back of each hand and along her forearms. Whatever else Loghry did to the woman, his blood kept her addicted to one of the most toxic flame drugs in Five Bridges, amethyst flame.

She shook her body back and forth and let out an ear-shattering shriek. Her long black hair hung down the front of her face showing only a portion of her eyes, nose and mouth. Her dark red dress was filthy.

He'd heard a kind of insanity could afflict vampires who grew addicted in this second-hand way.

Being one of her kind, he was horrified at what she'd become. Yet something about her drew him closer, maybe because she was a vampire, or maybe it was a kind of enthrallment the addiction caused. Flame drugs were highly unpredictable, and often showed different effects from one addict to another. He kept moving toward the woman.

"Vaughn, what is it?" Emma tracked with him.

When he was within three feet of the cell, the vampire stopped all her movements and stared at him. Slowly, she lowered her feet to the ground. She was tall, at least six feet, and had gray eyes.

She pushed one side of her hair away from her face, then the other. "Nathan?" His name came out on a harsh rasp. "Is that you?"

Vaughn recoiled. He sucked in a huge amount of air, then shouted long and loud, "No-o-o-o!"

~ ~ ~

Emma gripped Vaughn's arm. "What's going on? Who is she? What's wrong?"

Vaughn turned to Emma. "This woman is Beth. My sister."

Emma shifted to stare at the prisoner. "You mean, Loghry's had her all this time?"

Vaughn nodded.

Emma put her hand to her chest. "Oh, dear God."

The woman's wild movements had ceased, though she still clung to the bars of the cell with her hands. She bore a specific sign of a vampire who took blood from a drug-addicted host. The usual flame markings were broken up and had a spotty look, which meant she didn't take the drug herself. Even her bare wrists and arms showed the mottled flame markings. All of Five Bridges knew Loghry was addicted to amethyst flame.

A masculine voice called from across the central area of the labyrinth. "Well, Emma, isn't this a delightful coincidence? I brought Beth to Loghry, you stole the triplets from Loghry with Officer Vaughn's help, and now here's Vaughn's sister trapped in the labyrinth. It's as though we've all come full circle. Sometimes the *alter* life can be damn poetic."

Emma recognized Dagen's voice, but when she turned to scan the area, she couldn't see him. She drew close to Vaughn, but her hand went to the butt of her Sig.

Movement near the cage holding the teens drew Emma's gaze. Dagen stepped into one of the pale circles of light. He held an AR-15, supported by both hands.

Vaughn slowly turned to face Dagen. "You did this to my sister? You abducted Beth? But I watched vampires carry her into the air."

"What can I say? Those vampires owed me. Loghry wanted your sister, those men were in deep to him and I gave them a way out of the mess they'd made. Eventually, I had to kill them off, of course, because you were so persistent in your efforts to find your sister. Such remarkable sibling affection."

Dagen's gaze slid from Vaughn to Emma. "As for events of last night, Emma, you've finally worn out Loghry's patience and I can't protect you anymore." His nostrils flared. "I think you've been extremely foolish in choosing Vaughn because you and I could have become a real power couple in Five Bridges. Instead, your Border Patrol officer will never be able to keep you safe in our world. Very stupid, if you ask me."

"Nobody's asking."

"Your funeral."

She glanced at Vaughn. She could see he was still in shock about his sister's fate. He even turned away from Dagen and faced Beth once more.

But Beth had begun to climb the bars of the cell again, holding on with her toes and fingers then swinging wildly back and forth like an ape. She shrieked long and loud, making a sound Emma didn't think possible for a woman to utter, not even an *alter* female.

"Just ignore the vampire. I want your weapons in the dirt. Both of you. Now."

Emma ignored his order. She wanted the whole truth first because in this moment she didn't care if she lived or died. "Did you kill Max? And I'd appreciate a straight answer this time. After all, there's no reason not to tell me now."

Dagen's lips turned down. "That bastard was squeaky clean and the wrong kind of leader for our pack. I had no choice but to put him down."

Emma worked at breathing. She wanted to claw Dagen's face off, to hurt him, to destroy him. "He was a good man who wanted his pack to thrive. And he wanted at least part of Savage Territory not to be in league with the cartels or wizards like Loghry. He stood for something good, decent and honorable."

Dagen moved slowly in her direction, his rifle loose in his hands. He didn't seem worried at all and he definitely didn't care.

That's when Emma realized he'd brought a force with him. She could feel the warlocks drawing closer to the central cage area even as Dagen moved. "You understand so little about Five Bridges. Don't you get it, Emma? You would have died a long time ago if it weren't for me. Until tonight, Loghry has allowed you to keep breathing because I asked him to leave you alone. I see that surprises you. But do you honestly believe that Savage Territory is held together by honor among the packs?

Hah. I do a lot of favors and spend a helluva lot of money so that the cartels will allow us to roam our forests without injury.

"As for Loghry, the wizard has known you were a threat for a very long time, something having to do with his gift of prescience. That he values my service should tell you a lot. And despite his wish to get rid of you, he's allowing me to make you a final offer. You get one last chance. If you come with me now, you'll move to Savage and live with me. You'll submit to me. If not—" He gestured to the cage holding Beth. "You'll be food for Loghry's favorite pet."

Emma stared at Dagen, at the confident set of his shoulders and the way he held his chin high. He was a man in charge of the situation, holding both her life and Vaughn's in his sleazy hands. "You've been frank with me so let me return the favor. I'd rather eat shards of glass than spend a second as your woman. And that's the choice I make tonight. Have I made myself clear?"

Disgust drew Dagen's cheeks back. "You've looked down on me from the first. But it's Max who's dead, not me."

"Because you killed him, you bastard. So do whatever it is you're going to do. I won't submit to you, not now, not ever. Death would be preferable."

He stared at her for a long, hard moment. "You fucking bitch."

Those words brought Vaughn from his shocked out state. "How about you and I battle, right here, Dagen, and see who deserves Emma."

Dagen merely smiled. "We'll be batting all right, but it will be on my terms." He then lifted his hand and made a swirling gesture.

His troops poured into the space so fast, Emma didn't even have time to draw her Sig. Vaughn's Glock had just cleared his holster, when both she and Vaughn were shoved face down into the dirt from behind. A warlock had a knee in her back as he disarmed her and several more kept Vaughn pinned. One held fingers sizzling with power to the back of his head.

Don't move, Vaughn. The warlock has his killing energy lit up, his fingers poised behind your head.

I know. I can feel it. He started cursing aloud, calling Dagen all kinds of beautiful names. Dagen snorted and nodded to a nearby warlock, who in turn brought the butt of his rifle down hard on the back of Vaughn's head. His whole body went limp.

Dagen drew close and kicked dirt in Emma's face. "And you go in the cage, where you deserve to be."

Two warlocks lifted her to her feet in grips so tight all she could do was kick at them with her legs. But two more men grabbed her lower half so that she was now horizontal in the air.

As Dagen worked the cell lock, Beth began to shriek all over again. She leaped once more from the side bars of the cell to the front then to the other side.

Dagen delivered his orders. "As soon as I open the door, throw her inside."

When Beth was in the opposite corner, clinging to the bars with toes and fingers, Dagen flipped the door open. Before Beth could get near any of them, the men holding Emma threw her onto the floor.

She tumbled in the dirt, righting herself quickly, her gaze fixed on Beth. Using her peripheral vision, she could see that Dagen had ordered Vaughn to be removed from the central area of the labyrinth. It took all five warlocks to carry him out.

Dagen sneered. "I'm leaving the door unlocked in case you miraculously avoid your cellmate's fangs. Part of me hopes you escape then I can hunt you down. But good luck." He laughed as he disappeared down the passageway following after his force and Vaughn.

She was on her own now as Beth jumped from one barred cell wall to the next, her gaze fixed on Emma, her eyes manic as she stared at Emma's throat.

The triplets joined her in the cell, moving back and forth frenetically. *We don't know what to do or how to help.*

Emma reached into the future focusing on Vaughn and the triplets. A series of quick snapshots emerged. *Becca, find Vaughn. Be with him. He'll need you in this. You must remind him that we're a team. Tell him that. Tell him that he and I are a team.*

Becca nodded and the ghosts vanished.

Now for the other problem.

Emma had to try something. She shouted telepathically, hoping she could make contact with the woman. *Beth! I'm a friend of Vaughn's! Can you hear me? Understand me?*

But the minute or so of clear-mindedness that Beth had experienced earlier, when she'd first recognized her brother, had long since ended. The dementia from a steady diet of amethyst-tainted blood had taken over again.

Beth leaped from the cell bars once more, only this time she landed on the dirt floor. She hunched over as she moved, her arms dragging lower and lower, her hands in the shapes of claws. Her eyes were red-rimmed and blazed with hunger. They'd darkened as well and no longer looked gray, like Vaughn's. Her fangs made a sudden frightening appearance.

Emma jumped to her feet, intent on bolting for the door. But Beth sprang, knocking Emma flat on her back. Before Emma could prevent the attack, Beth bit hard, tearing into Emma's throat.

She cried out in pain and started to struggle, but the moment Beth began to suck down Emma's blood, Emma fell into a deeply enthralled state. Her body grew completely lax and her mind fell into a sublime state of peace, the tearing of her skin and vein a distant agony.

Emma wondered if this was how she would die, with Vaughn's sister, demented because of a second-hand addiction to amethyst flame and drinking her to death.

~ ~ ~

Vaughn awoke suddenly when a wave of cold water hit the back of his head. For a few long seconds, he couldn't remember where he was or what had happened to him. But the memories rushed back swiftly. He and Emma had been knocked to the ground and something had smashed into his skull.

"Emma." His voice was hoarse.

"Calling out for your girlfriend? She can't help you now. She can't even help herself."

Dagen, again. "Fuck you."

A boot kicked Vaughn hard in the ribs, the reinforced steel crunching a couple of his ribs. He grunted in pain as Dagen moved closer to his face. All Vaughn could see was a pair of dusty shitkickers. The low light and a view of diverging paths a few yards away, told Vaughn he was still in the labyrinth. His head hurt like hell. He forced himself to begin the healing process, but it would take forever at this rate.

"Where's Emma? What did you do to her?" The broken ribs made it hard to breathe then to get the words out.

"She's with Beth, of course. Your sister is no doubt feeding on Emma right now, drinking from her vein. Again, another piece of Five Bridges's poetry. Unfortunately, Emma will be dead soon. Not your sister, of course. She's Loghry's pet, so she'll live on and on. Did you know Loghry let's Beth feed from his vein? Of course you do. It's part of the charm of the whole picture."

Vaughn didn't answer him.

"On your feet." Dagen spoke sharply, his voice echoing through the small space.

Vaughn rose up, but struggled to get his weight over his knees. His head ached from the concussion and his ribs were killing him. Though he could eventually fix himself up with his vampire healing, it would take hours. Right now, however, he had only minutes.

When he finally stood upright, five warlocks surrounded him. Dagen, the only shifter present, stood directly in front of him. He no longer held his AR-15.

Dagen had small dark eyes and a vicious face, the latter no doubt hardened from his experience as an *alter* shifter in Savage Territory. He was a couple of inches shorter than either Vaughn or the powerful warlocks who surrounded him. But he had complete command of the situation.

"What do you want, Dagen?"

"I want you running for your life through the labyrinth, like all the other frightened rabbits I've chased over the years. If you're clever, you might even find your way back to Emma. First, though, I intend to give myself a small advantage."

Before Vaughn knew what Dagen meant to do, something metal hit

Vaughn hard at the back of his knee. He heard the bone crunch and at the same time he fell, rolling to the side. He gripped his leg and gritted his teeth. But despite his attempts to hold it in, an anguished sound came out of his throat.

Through waves of pain, he watched Dagen and his force of five warlocks disappear down different paths, until he was alone. Because of his ribs, each breath was a struggle. Was he going to die like a wounded animal in Loghry's maze?

Emma came to mind. Somehow, he had to get back to her, had to save her from Beth's mania. But he had broken ribs, a shattered knee, and six men ready to do more damage no matter which route he took.

Worse, he had no idea where he was in relation to the central part of the labyrinth or how far away Beth's cell might be. He had to try. He forced himself to stand up.

The moment he hobbled in the direction of the nearest path, however, one of the warlocks rushed him, punching him hard in the gut, afterward disappearing.

With the wind knocked out of him, Vaughn slumped to the dirt again, rolling once more onto his side to avoid landing on his shattered knee.

For one of the few times in his life, Vaughn had no idea what the fuck he should do. But it was clear that if he remained where he was, he'd be slowly beaten to death. Physical strength wouldn't get him out of this situation and his healing ability sucked given the dire nature of his injuries.

But he had to figure this out. He had two women counting on him. If he stayed as he was, both he and Emma would die and Beth would remain Loghry's slave for years to come.

He scooted himself backward to lean against the wall of the passageway. His leg was on fire and it was taking him time to catch his breath. Every draw on his lungs hurt.

His thoughts kept rolling toward Emma and his certainty that his sister was slowly draining her to death. But what good would it do for him to focus on Emma?

Yet no matter how hard he tried, he couldn't keep his thoughts away from her. He'd dreaded this moment from the time he'd started caring about her because there was no way he could help her now. He was physically incapable of even getting to her.

Vaughn?

He sat up a little straighter. *Emma? You sound so faint.*

I'm drifting away here. I just want you to know … that I love you … and I'm so sorry about Beth. No other words followed.

Emma? He tried contacting her several more times, but heard nothing in response.

Emma!

Nothing.

So Dagen was right and Emma was being drained to death.

He was stuck in the labyrinth, his body broken, the woman he loved dying, and not a damn thing he could do about it. He felt as he had when he'd seen Beth abducted right in front of his house with no way to save her. This was the reason he'd avoided any kind of closeness, why he'd held back from Emma. He'd never wanted to feel this way again, the complete impotence of being unable to save someone he loved.

The triplets suddenly appeared, floating in the air in front of him. They swayed back and forth and a strange mournful sound filled the air.

He felt in his bones that Emma had sent the ghosts to him. But why? What could three spirits do to help in this situation?

Becca, can you talk to me?

Her eyes popped wide. *Yes. Yes. Yes.*

Did Emma send you?

Becca nodded. *She was searching the future and said we must be with you, to help you.*

Did she say in what way?

She wanted us to remind you that you're a team, you and Emma.

Vaughn didn't think this was much help at all. *Was that it? She didn't say anything else?*

Becca's face twisted in anguish. *No, only that she wanted you to remember that you're a team. Is there anything we can do?*

Let me think.

Vaughn stared at the ghosts for a long time, his hand to his ribs, holding them in place while he took each breath. He shook from the pain, which didn't help.

So, what had Emma been trying to tell him?

Emma's abilities had brought the triplets back into their lives. She'd helped them escape their bodies in the Graveyard and she'd encouraged their presence in her home.

He loved that about Emma, that she was generous with her heart and her time. Helping the girls initially almost got her killed because he and Emma had stayed with them way too long.

She'd given Vaughn so much in the short time he'd known her. She'd become a friend, a good friend. He'd treasured their phone conversations. Each one had eased his heart.

Emma had made Five Bridges tolerable. That's what she'd done for him. She'd done the same for these three young ghosts. And he didn't want her to die. Dammit, the woman deserved to live.

But she'd done something more as well. She'd reached into the darkest place of his heart and filled it with hope. Her love had made him feel like Five Bridges was a place he wanted to be.

It was Emma. Always Emma.

That's when he realized that she had truly changed everything for him, just as she had for these ghosts.

Vaughn? Becca looked worried.

Emma's the key. She sent you here to help me see that.

His thoughts flew back to the gun battle against Loghry and his forces in Savage Territory. Vaughn had gotten hit, his shin bone shattered. Then Emma had healed him with her witch power.

She'd healed him.

She'd healed him.

For whatever reason, from the time they'd come together, they'd actually shared their powers. His presence in her spellroom had enhanced Emma's abilities. She could now levitate because of him and she could reach into the future.

He could fly faster now and see ghosts when he never could before. But he wondered if there was something else he could do. Could he utilize her profound healing ability?

He looked down at his wrecked knee and put both hands around it. Was it possible? Could he make use of Emma's healing gift and restore his broken body in time to save himself as well as Emma and Beth?

He turned every thought to Emma and her *alter* witch gifts.

As he did, small jolts of electricity began flowing down his arms and into his hands and fingers. And just like that, healing began to work on his knee at lightning speed. The more he focused, the stronger the wave became. Only it didn't just heal his knee, but began to flow through his body to his ribs and higher to repair the ache in his head.

After a few more seconds, he could breathe easily and the throbbing in his ribs and his knee began to drift away.

You look better. Becca clapped her hands together, though there was no accompanying sound.

He met her gaze and smiled. *I am, and you've helped me tremendously by delivering Emma's message. But I want you to go be with her now. I've got this.*

Becca grinned and the three ghosts vanished.

As Vaughn let the last of the healing process take him over, he thought of Dagen and the warlocks waiting for him. Vaughn knew he couldn't defeat them with only his fully-restored physical strength.

He needed another advantage.

He needed Emma's other gift, the one that had led them to reach the center of the labyrinth in the first place. She could see snapshots of the future which meant there was a strong possibility he'd be able to access similar images as well. In order to make it back to Emma in one piece, he'd have to know what his opponents would do in the immediate future, how each would attack him.

He heard voices moving in his direction. They weren't far away.

His vampire hearing picked up the words. "He's just sitting there."

"Then let's cut him up. I'd like to see the vampire bastard bleed."

Vaughn focused on Emma and the future. The snapshots appeared quickly and began to flow in a steady stream.

Fully healed, he leaped to his feet. The snapshots showed him what he needed to do moment-by-moment.

He levitated to the ceiling and drew his knees up tight to his chest. A warlock flew hard across the space below Vaughn. He would have knocked Vaughn to the ground otherwise, or worse, since the warlock carried a sword.

Instead, he landed square against the stone wall where Vaughn had been sitting.

The sound of a bone snapping, confirmed the next set of images that showed the warlock face down on the ground, his neck broken.

As Vaughn lowered himself to the dirt, he kept the future snapshots moving swiftly. The second attacker would arrive within seconds. Vaughn shifted to a horizontal position at the same time that a sword flew through the air sliding well above his body. The sword clattered against the wall, but if Vaughn hadn't moved, it would have caught his upper torso.

Vaughn glanced at the next few snapshots, dove for the sword, grabbed it by the handle, then levitated toward the far right pathway at the same time that the second warlock shouted and lunged toward him. But Vaughn was faster because of the vision. He sliced upward in a diagonal thrust, caught the warlock in the abdomen and stabbed him through to the spine.

The man screamed and fell, then writhed in the dirt.

Vaughn caught the next set of images and darted down the same pathway from which the warlock had emerged. Because of the vision, he knew where he was headed. He levitated swiftly.

The snapshots showed the third warlock, sword in hand, at the next intersection. When Vaughn arrived, he pulled his knees up, then kicked out hard. He caught the warlock in the back, shoved with all his might and slammed the man against the stone wall. He slumped to the dirt, his head bashed in, blood everywhere.

Vaughn held tight to the snapshots, keeping them flowing so that he could follow the path back to Emma. Three warlocks down, two to go, plus a psychopathic shifter.

He was getting closer to the center of the labyrinth, but would he find Emma alive?

CHAPTER SEVEN

Emma's breathing was shallow as Beth continued to savage her neck. Though held in a thrall and unable to move, tears dripped down the sides of Emma's face and into her hair. The nearness of her death was almost unbearable.

Her thoughts were all for Vaughn and how much she loved him. She couldn't believe this miracle had happened. She'd never thought to know love after Max died, but she didn't want Vaughn to die, and she really didn't want Beth to remain imprisoned in Loghry's underground labyrinth.

But what could she do? A demented vampire held her in thrall and was steadily draining her to death.

What's your name? The voice was female and it took Emma a moment to realize Beth had contacted her telepathically.

My name is Emma. Is that you, Beth?

Yes. You taste so good. I can't stop. It's the amethyst drug forcing me to keep going. I'm sorry.

Yet you can communicate with me. Is your mind clearing?

Yes, but I still can't stop. When I drink from Loghry, he has his servants beat me until I release his neck.

For the first time since Dagen had thrown her in Beth's cell, Emma began to hope. If her blood was helping Beth, then maybe something else could be done for the vampire.

She thought about her time with Vaughn, how much her witch powers had increased, especially her ability to heal. Maybe she could send a kind of healing to Beth that would break the addiction's hold on her.

127

She was sure as hell going to try.

Once more, as she had the first time she'd seen the three ghosts in the Graveyard, she opened herself up to all that she was in the *alter* world. Only this time, she focused on the ways she was connected to Vaughn and how he enhanced the abilities she possessed.

The emerging sensations felt like a wave of power she'd never known before. She centered that power on her healing gift then let it flood her veins.

After a few seconds, Beth's voice entered Emma's mind again. *What is that? Your blood tastes different and I'm feeling dizzy now.*

I'm sending you as much healing as I can.

Thank you. It's wonderful, but I still can't release you. I'm so sorry.

Emma remembered something else as well, that she and Vaughn were in a strange place of being able to share their powers with each other. She focused on Vaughn's vampire nature and could actually feel it coming forward. Some vampires could enthrall other vampires, but not if they were weak like Beth.

As Emma experienced Vaughn's vampire power, she found Beth's thrall breaking up. The moment she was able to lift her arm, she placed her hand on top of Beth's head. Her healing then flowed straight into Beth's mind.

I don't know what you're doing, but keep doing it. My compulsion to continue drinking from you is fading.

A moment later, Beth drew back from Emma's throat. "Oh, my God, I've torn you to pieces." She leaned close and used her tongue to help seal the wounds. Emma did the rest as she sent healing to her neck as well.

After a moment, Beth sat back on her knees and stared at Emma's throat. "It's healed." She then put her hands on her head. "I can't believe this. I can think again."

Emma felt dizzy from the loss of so much blood, but she knew her body was quickly replenishing what she needed. She could also feel that Beth teetered on the edge of madness still.

She forced herself to her knees and this time planted both hands on Beth's head. The vampire moaned. "Thank you. Thank you so much. You've saved me."

"Beth, look at your skin. The flames are disappearing."

"My God." Beth drew in a ragged breath and tears began to flow down her cheeks. "The drugs have started to leave my system." She pressed her hands to her chest. "For the first time in years, I almost feel normal again."

"I have to stop now, Beth. I'm dizzy from what you took from me. I need to focus more of that healing on myself."

"Yes, of course." Beth swiped at more of her tears.

Emma closed her eyes and centered her healing power within her body. The sensation was close to miraculous as she regained her strength with each passing second. When she felt better, her thoughts turned to Vaughn and her need to go to him. She rose to her feet and at the same time, she became aware of the ghosts in the cell.

Becca's voice entered her mind. *Emma, you made it.*

I did. But how is Vaughn? Is he—? She couldn't form the rest of the words.

He'd started to heal himself when he sent us to you. He looked much better, but that's all we know. Dagen and his men were waiting in the shadows to hurt him.

Emma glanced at the teens still huddled in the cage across the way.

Beth joined her. "Loghry has brought hundreds of girls to this place over the years. He would chase them through the labyrinth. I watched so many die and there was nothing I could do."

Emma turned to her. "We can do something now. Dagen left the door unlocked. What do you say we take these girls then get the hell out of here?"

Beth nodded, but compressed her lips. Tears rolled down her cheeks once more. She glanced down at the dirt and levitated, though very slowly. "I haven't been able to do this for years. Not for years. That drug was a nightmare."

Emma felt the urgency to leave, but she needed to give Beth a moment to get used to being sane again. She patted her shoulder. "Keep practicing. You'll need to be ready to move swiftly." She pushed the door wide. "I'm going to contact your brother."

"Okay."

Vaughn, can you hear me?

Emma, you're alive! Thank God. Listen to me, I've taken down the five warlocks. It's now me and Dagen, and I've been accessing the snapshot visions, sharing your power. You're in the images now. Will you do what I tell you?

Absolutely.

Good. I'm less than a minute out and Dagen is right behind me. I've had to weave my way through the maze to get to you, but I'm heading in your direction. You'll need to get to your gun.

I'm on it.

Emma found her handgun a few yards away to the right of the cell. She picked it up and told Beth to come to her, to get behind her. Beth, still levitating, moved in place. Emma directed her thoughts once more to Vaughn. *I've got my Sig.*

Sorry, Em, but the snapshots indicate you'll need to shoot Dagen.

I don't have a problem with that. In her line of work, she'd taken down a lot of bad guys.

We're almost there. Shit, the images have been blocked.

It's Loghry. He probably figured out what you were doing. I'll take over. Do you have enough information to get to the center of the maze?

Yes.

She added one last thought. *Your Glock is on the ground to the left of the cell.*

Got it.

She addressed Beth, reaching her telepathically. She didn't want Loghry to actually hear anything they were planning, *Beth, I'm going to access the future. Stay put and follow my lead, can you do that?*

Yes.

Just stick close.

She opened herself up to the snapshots that created a vision of the future.

They came quickly, showing her she had only a few seconds to prepare. *Beth, stay behind me.*

I will.

She switched to contact Vaughn. *I've got the future. You're only ten seconds away. Take a left then a right.*

Don't worry, Em. I can sense where you are now.

We're ready.

Emma saw what she had to do, and she counted down for Beth. *Three … two … one …*

The next moment, Vaughn shot through the space, flying past them. Suddenly, Dagen was there, just a few feet away, his AR-15 rising.

Emma pulled the trigger and fired straight into Dagen's torso. He flew backward onto the dirt, a hole in his chest, blood pouring. Still he lifted his rifle. She fired repeatedly but the arm kept rising. The bastard had power.

Vaughn drew up next to her, his Glock in hand, and fired one bullet into Dagen's skull. His arm finally fell back harmlessly, and the rifle dropped into the dirt.

Silence followed, except for Vaughn's rough breathing. It was clear he'd been battling hard. She turned to him. He put his arm around her, and she pivoted to grab him around the waist. He drew her tight against him and hugged her.

A sob caught in her throat. "I thought we were both dead."

"We made it, Emma. But we're not done yet."

"Nathan?" Emma heard Beth call her brother's name. She released Vaughn.

Releasing Emma, he turned in Beth's direction. "You're back and the amethyst flames on your skin are gone. What happened?"

Beth smiled, her eyes tearing up. "Emma healed me. That's how we got out of this. It was all Emma."

Vaughn held his arms wide and Beth flew into them. He met Emma's gaze over his sister's head. "Thank you."

Emma nodded but she lifted a finger and slid into telepathy. *We've got to get out of here. I can feel Loghry's presence and I have a strong sense he was able to watch everything that just happened. In fact, I'm sure of it. I'll access the future again.*

Vaughn nodded. *I think he can only disrupt the snapshots for one of us at a time, so let me know if he blocks you, and I'll take over.*

She nodded. *We'll do this by flowing back and forth.*

He held her gaze for a moment, carefully shifting Beth to one side, then opening his free arm to her. When she drew close, he surrounded her with his arm then leaned down to kiss her. "I know. We're a team."

Emma's heart fluttered because of what she saw in his eyes. He was with her now, really with her, nothing held back. She drew a deep breath. "We're a team. Now let's get your sister and these other girls out of here."

"I love you, Em."

"I love you, too."

~ ~ ~

Vaughn focused tightly on Emma and held his mind open. Though he tried to access the snapshot images, again, he couldn't see a damn thing, which meant Loghry was still blocking him. But he knew Emma was working to engage the future again as well.

After a moment, Emma dipped her chin. *I've seen what we do next. We need to get the girls and head back through the labyrinth the way we came. I've seen Brannick in place, waiting.*

She turned as she spoke, then gestured for Beth to follow. He moved in behind his sister as all three of them levitated swiftly to the opposite cage.

I'll contact Brannick. He thought about using his phone but he didn't want Loghry to know what he was up to. He tapped on Brannick's telepathy.

When Brannick responded, Vaughn told him they were coming out with five girls who would need to be carried to safety.

My team's ready.

Knew I could count on you. Vaughn smiled as he broke off the communication. He watched Emma pull the rod from the cell door's locking mechanism, a simple arrangement located far enough on the outside that the girls would never be able to reach it. With the rod gone, Emma pulled the door wide.

She waved to the girls. "Come with us. We're getting you out of here." The girls rose uneasily to their feet.

Emma went into the cell and spoke quietly to them, then turned back to Vaughn, frowning. Her voice once more pierced his mind. *The images are blocked again. Your turn.*

I'll take it from here.

Vaughn opened the shared witch power and the future images slid straight into his head. He knew the route he needed to take to get the girls out and let Emma know what was going on. He felt compelled to add, *But Loghry's here, in the labyrinth just as you said. I can feel him now.*

With her arm supporting one of the girls, Emma caught his gaze and nodded to him. *Me, too. So, let's go.*

He watched her turn to the teens. She held a finger to her lips, making sure each of them understood they should be very quiet.

A solemn hush came over the girls, and those that had been weeping, drew shuddering breaths and wiped their faces.

Vaughn told Beth to track right behind him. He needed to know she was safe.

He glanced at Emma. *We need to move fast, Em. Tell the girls.*

"We'll be running. Follow Vaughn. I'll be behind you all. Now, go."

Maybe it was the girls' basic survival instinct, but they lined up behind Vaughn, and the moment he levitated, they charged after him. They didn't even balk at the sight of Dagen's corpse near the exit point.

He could hear Emma encouraging them from behind. One last glance over his shoulder told him Beth was up to the challenge as well. She was levitating with confidence.

Vaughn moved quickly into the maze. At the first juncture, he gave Emma the directions telepathically, then contacted Brannick in the same way, alerting him they were on the way.

Brannick confirmed that he would meet up with Vaughn and the teens at the back of the guest house. Brannick and his team were less than a minute out, and the night sky was clear of any other *alter* species in flight.

Vaughn could almost breathe easily now.

The route back to the entrance was circuitous, but the images remained sharp. He moved at a brisk clip, with one eye on those behind him to make sure Emma, Beth and the girls stuck close. The teens seemed to understand they were being ushered to safety, and their intense effort to keep up with Vaughn gave him the confidence to pick up the pace a little more.

Every second counted.

He could also feel the wizard hunting them, the dark nature of the beast spilling his evil intentions throughout the labyrinth. Suddenly, Vaughn grew dizzy and his steps started to slow.

But the next moment, Emma was beside him. She put a hand on his forehead. *Loghry has spread a spell through the labyrinth. This should help.*

Vaughn's mind began to clear, enough to engage the images, then the future was blocked again. *Emma, you'll have to take the lead.*

He loved that Emma didn't hesitate. He watched her shift focus, and he saw the moment she'd re-engaged the vision snapshots.

Her voice sped through his mind. *Get to the rear. I'll lead the girls out. We're almost there, even though the spell makes it feel like we're miles from the exit door.*

Vaughn nodded, then let the girls pass. He saw that Beth was shaking, and he slid his arm around her. He was pretty sure her body was caught in a withdrawal from amethyst flame.

A couple more turns, however, and the dizziness started taking over his mind again. He kept pushing his feet forward, trailing after the last girl, but it wasn't long before his ankles grew leaden and his mind clouded once more. "Sorry, Beth."

"I'm feeling it, too. It's Loghry."

Vaughn contacted Emma. *Loghry's spell has me. Can't move. Can't think. Beth is with me, she's very sick and the spell has her, as well. Get the girls to Brannick if you can.*

I will and Vaughn, I'll come back to you as fast as I can.

I know you will.

But even as he slumped to the dirt, with Beth falling into his arms, he held his mind and his power open to Emma. He felt in his bones that somehow she'd be able to make use of all that he was as a vampire and return to him.

Beth shook badly now, caught in a severe withdrawal.

Vaughn tried to access Emma's healing power, but Loghry's spell prevented him.

Suddenly, Loghry arrived, floating into the space. Vaughn could smell the darkness in him, a stench that turned his stomach. He was tall and levitated as the more powerful spellcasters could. He wore a black fringed scarf wrapped around his neck as well as a black, long-sleeved, leather coat to hide his addiction to amethyst flame.

His eyes were black and sunken, his skin white as chalk, the way Emma had described him from her nightmares. His cheekbones were pronounced and skeletal, his nose slightly bulbous, and his lips thick and violet colored. He barely looked like a man anymore. Maybe he hadn't been one in a long time. His evil temperament coupled with amethyst flame had given him the appearance of the monster he was.

"I should kill you right now, Officer Vaughn. Your sister with you. But I'll wait, because first I want you to watch your woman die."

~ ~ ~

Emma knew what she had to do, but it killed her not to immediately go back for Vaughn and Beth.

Instead, she broke through the final veil of the spell that Loghry had set in place at the exit. Sure enough, the stone stairs leading to the outside appeared right in front of her.

She gestured for the girls to climb the stairs. "Hurry! Go with the men at the top."

Brannick was right there, urging each forward as well. "Come on, girls. We've got you. Let's get you home."

He even ran down several steps, picked the first girl up, then levitated her to ground level. He passed her quickly to one of his men, then drew the next forward.

At the base of the stairs, tears filled Emma's eyes as she watched each girl being carried into the air to safety.

Brannick had the last girl in his arms, but he didn't take off right away. *Where's Vaughn?*

I'm going back for him.

Emma, what's wrong? Should I stay?

She smiled suddenly. *No. I've got this.*

Brannick offered her a crooked smile in return. *Do your worst, witch. I suspect Loghry's in for a surprise.*

Emma grinned as he took off. Whatever happened next, they'd done it. They'd saved another group of girls, and she vowed that so long as she lived, she'd spend the rest of her life getting innocent humans out of Five Bridges.

She turned toward the entrance to the labyrinth, then opened her ability to see the immediate future, but static returned. Loghry was blocking her.

It didn't matter, though, because she could feel Vaughn now, like a second skin. His vampire strength surrounded her and she drew his energy close. This was something Loghry couldn't disrupt.

Keeping her mind focused on Vaughn, she began making her way through the labyrinth.

The path was as clear to her as if she'd seen it in a series of snapshots.

But she could feel Loghry as well. Maybe it was her connection to Vaughn, but he seemed more sinister than ever.

As she moved, she felt Loghry approach her telepathy, but she blocked him. She didn't want the wizard inside her head. She took several pathways to finally enter the space where Loghry held Vaughn captive.

Vaughn's eyes looked glazed. He was still caught in Loghry's spell. As for Beth, though Vaughn held her close, she shook head to toe.

Loghry stood off to the side, his lips curved as he stared at Emma. He was as tall as Vaughn, though emaciated as addicts often were. His lips were actually the color of the drug he took.

"So we meet at last, Emma. I've seen you numerous times in the visions I occasionally enjoyed, and of course I met you in your dreams earlier. But you should know that I've prepared for your arrival. You don't equal me in power."

Emma didn't respond because that's exactly what he wanted her to do.

When she felt him press on her telepathy again, she blocked him as she had before.

"Very good." He inclined his head slightly, an acknowledgment of her power.

He began to unwind the black scarf, though at first she wasn't sure why. But when he completed the process and let it fall to the dirt, she realized he'd wanted to knock her out of her stride. He almost succeeded, because she couldn't believe the state of his throat and neck. Everyone thought he used the scarf to cover up his addiction. Instead, the fabric had been hiding the bruising up and down his throat as well as a large number of feeding scars where Beth had done permanent damage through the years.

At the same time that her gaze became fixed to the horror of his wounds, she felt a wave of energy come from Loghry. She felt dizzy and nauseous, then she understood. He was using the disgusting nature of his scars to distract her while he applied his spell.

She gave herself a shake and met his gaze once more. "Not gonna work." She conjured a spell of her own, full of light and warmth and flung it at him with a wave of her own energy.

He lifted an arm and squinted. He even shouted as though in pain. He might have tremendous ability, but he still had feet of clay.

Despite the fact that she stayed focused on her spell, she felt Loghry battle back swiftly, and like a shower of glitter in the air, her counter-spell disappeared.

"I'm angry with you, Emma. Though more so at Dagen for putting you in with my pet. He should have known your blood might have the ability to heal Beth. The truth is that I could have stopped you from killing the shifter, but he and I had gone as far as we could go."

"You're a monster, Loghry."

"Please, let's not reduce ourselves to name-calling. Especially since I have an offer for you, though essentially it's the same one Dagen made. I want you to join with me, both sexually, of course, and with all the latent power you've been suppressing. You're a woman of exceptional abilities and we could accomplish extraordinary things together. In fact, we could rule Five Bridges. Think what that could mean." His gaze fell the full length of her body, then back up. "Of course, you would need to embrace amethyst flame."

"And I'll give you the same answer I gave Dagen: I'd rather eat sharp pieces of glass."

"That can't be your only answer. Don't you see? You've got the wrong attitude about living here. I was like you early on, wanting to retain my humanity, hoping perhaps I could do some good in Five Bridges. But I was attacked by vampires after only being here a few months. They were officers of the Crescent Border Patrol. Your boyfriend was one of them, which was why I took Beth. Vaughn robbed me of hope and I decided to do the same for him. I knew abducting his sister would cause him a lot more anguish than if I merely killed him straight out."

Emma snorted. "Funny how Vaughn remembers the night you were attacked very differently from your account, or have you forgotten that you killed a woman, a female vampire?"

He spread his hands wide. "It was an accident."

"How is using your bare hands for several minutes to strangle a woman to death anything like 'an accident'." She couldn't help herself; she made air quotes.

"Well, it was. I was caught up in the drug. I tried to tell the men, but they were intent on doing me harm. And for that, they needed to be punished."

Loghry clearly enjoyed rewriting events to suit himself.

He smiled. "Of course it turned out brilliantly since they thought I was dead. It had been so easy to fool them and even easier to leave the morgue."

"But why did you have to abduct and kill all those girls?"

He shrugged. "I was merely taking my revenge, that's all, for being attacked. Vaughn and his friends are to blame."

"You're full of shit, you know that? You see yourself as a victim which you've then used as an excuse for doing whatever the hell you want. You enjoy being an addict and you get off on torture and murder. You can call it revenge, if you like. But in my book, you're just a run of the mill psychopath."

"More name-calling?" He moved in her direction, one slow step at a time.

As he grew closer, she felt a new spell descend like a warm blanket over her body. Her emotions evened out as though spilling over sand and disappearing between the grains.

"Feeling better, Emma?"

He was suddenly right in front of her, though she hadn't seen him move. Some distant part of her mind knew she was in danger, but the rest of her felt at peace. She'd thought Loghry would breathe fire and burn her to a crisp. Instead, he was easing her fears and making her feel wonderful.

"I want you with me, Emma. You have so much to offer." He stroked her hair. She longed for him to touch her, to do anything he wanted. "And I can make it so that you always feel desire for me."

Emma struggled deep within herself. She needed to break free of Loghry's thrall, but no matter how fiercely she called on her witchy powers, she couldn't do it.

CHAPTER EIGHT

Vaughn stared up at the wizard touching Emma. The man's long bony fingers glided the length of her hair, all the way down her back. He knew Loghry's spell held him in a state of thrall, yet each movement of the wizard's hand sparked Vaughn's rage.

He'd listened to the man's excuse for how he'd come to embrace his dark side. He'd spoken of his innocence as though there'd been a time when he was good and just. But Emma was right, the man was full of shit.

But it was his command over Emma that forced Vaughn to fight his way out of the spell. Yet, instead of summoning any of his vampire abilities, he focused on Emma's powers as a witch. The more he concentrated, the more he could feel a kind of barrier rising. It also helped that given Emma's level of power, Loghry was forced to work hard to bespell her. No doubt he was employing the full scope of his dark arts to keep her in an enthralled state, which might work for Vaughn.

He remained sitting where he was. Though it was risky, he contacted her telepathically. *Emma? Can you hear me?*

Yes. Oh, God, Vaughn, I can't break his hold over me. He's too powerful.

Think like a vampire, not a witch.

He watched her blink, a good sign.

Okay, like a vampire.

Beth drew back from Vaughn and slid off his lap to sit in the dirt. At the same time, she tapped against his telepathy, and he opened to her. *What is it, Beth?*

140

I can see that Emma shares our vampire gifts. She should bite Loghry. Tell her to bite his throat. She can enthrall him if she does.

The last thing Vaughn wanted was for Emma to engage with Loghry. But Beth was right. Emma might be able to enthrall the wizard if she could get to his neck. She was several inches shorter and it would be difficult, but if Vaughn was able to distract the wizard, it could work.

Emma, listen. You need to attack Loghry at his throat. Beth and I both believe you'd be able to enthrall him as only a vampire can. He probably doesn't realize how much we're sharing powers.

I don't know. I'm afraid if I made a move, he'd figure out what I was doing and block the strike.

I've thought about that. I intend to distract him, but you'll have to wait for my signal and be very quick. Can you do this?

There was a pause before she responded. *Yes, I can.* She sounded more confident.

Let me gain his attention, then I'll give you a count of three. Okay?

Go for it.

Vaughn knew the blocking spell he'd just built would give him the exact tool he needed right now to disrupt Loghry's concentration.

He called out in a strong voice, "You're a small man, aren't you, Loghry, attacking women. What is it? You afraid to battle a man?"

Loghry turned his head in Vaughn's direction. He didn't seem disturbed at all by Vaughn's words. He simply lifted his arm, and his dark energy flowed toward Vaughn, the same kind of electricity that the spellcasters could focus at the end of their fingers to kill other species.

But Vaughn's spell was now firmly in place and the stream of energy didn't touch him. In fact, he knew what he needed to do to distract Loghry.

He slowly stood up, and the wizard's brows rose. "How are you doing that?"

"Don't you know? Haven't you wondered why Emma and I have made it this far? Why I could block your power just now?"

At that, Loghry frowned. "You're making no sense."

Vaughn let Loghry stew as he contacted Emma. *Can you do it, Em? Has his thrall loosened enough?*

Yes, I can feel it easing up.

Then we'll give it a shot. Be ready on three.

I'm ready.

Loghry flared his nostrils. "Answer me! What are you talking about?" In this moment, Vaughn knew he had the wizard. "Because of Emma, of course. We've been sharing our powers."

"The fuck you have." Loghry scowled and lifted his arm once more in Vaughn's direction. "Let's see how you can handle this."

Vaughn could feel Loghry loading his power into his arm. He also knew gathering that power would take the time Emma needed to attack.

He started the countdown. *This is it, Emma. Three ... two ... one ... take him down!*

Emma moved vampire fast, levitating to sling an arm around Loghry's neck. She took his throat between her teeth. She didn't have fangs, but she held on. At the same time, Loghry grew very still.

Vaughn had worried that Loghry would fight. Instead, the wizard couldn't seem to move and his black eyes had filled with panic. Emma had him!

Vaughn moved swiftly to support Emma's hold on Loghry, holding her waist with his hands. "You've got him. Draw blood if you can."

Emma bit harder, and Vaughn watched a red stream glide down Loghry's neck. "Good. That's it."

Vaughn, I won't be able to hold him for long. Loghry's building his power from within. I'm slipping. I'm not vampire enough.

Vaughn could feel it as well, that Loghry had started regaining his power.

Suddenly, the wizard twisted his neck, and he felt Emma lose her grip. Loghry then released a wave of power that sent Vaughn and Emma flying backward and landing hard on the dirt floor near the stone wall.

Furious, Loghry moved to stand over them, his eyes blazing with hatred and madness. He lifted his arms, conjuring a new spell, then let his wizard power blast them, this time with a different be-spelled power.

The force of the new spell, full of electric energy, sent needle-like sensations over every inch of Vaughn's skin. The pain was so intense he writhed, Emma with him.

"So you thought you could take me, a dark wizard with more essential power than the pair of you could ever dream of." He waved his arms again, and the air grew thick and dense as though filled with black smoke.

Vaughn couldn't breathe. He heard Emma gasping for air as well. *Hold on, Em.*

I'm doing the best I can. But this hurts like anything and there's no oxygen.

I know.

Vaughn tried to rebuild the blocking spell, but couldn't. The pain intensified.

Vaughn, he's too powerful, and nothing I'm doing is working.

Suddenly, however, the spell broke, though Vaughn had no idea why.

He lifted up on his elbows and saw to his surprise that Beth had leaped on Loghry's back, her fangs sunk deep into his neck. She was drinking, which helped to solidify the thrall. But at the same time, blood poured from the wound as she continued to savage him. She'd sliced through his vein. Held in this state, Loghry would soon bleed to death.

A vampire could always enthrall a spellcaster, even a powerful wizard.

Loghry slumped to his knees, his leather coat flaring around him, but Beth held on tight. She kept him upright as blood ran down his coat and began pooling in the dirt. The wizard couldn't move a muscle, and he couldn't stop Beth.

Vaughn contacted her. *Do you need me to do anything, Beth?*

No. And if you try to interfere, you could break the thrall. Besides, he's mine. For what he did to me and all those girls, he's mine.

Vaughn turned his attention to Emma who moaned, but didn't open her eyes. He put his hand on top of her head and using her witch power, let the healing flow. Her whole body relaxed and after a minute, she was able to sit up.

She recoiled, however, at the horrible sight of Beth draining the life out of Loghry. "What should we do?"

"Beth said if we do anything we'll disrupt the thrall. And she wants this."

With both of them sitting in the dirt, Emma slipped her arm through his. "This is the least she deserves, isn't it? Yet for what she had to endure, it doesn't seem like enough."

"No, it doesn't."

A few minutes later, Beth released Loghry, and he fell forward in the dirt, his eyes open. He wasn't breathing, and the dirt all around him was stained with his blood.

At the same time, the triplets appeared nearby, staring down at the man who had tortured them and taken their lives.

"Look at the girls," Emma whispered. "I've never seen them so somber before."

"They're waiting for their killer."

"They must be."

Vaughn rose to his feet and lifted her with him. Beth was sitting against the opposite wall, shaking with exhaustion. The recent intake of more of Loghry's corrupt blood had caused some of the mottled flames to reappear on her neck and face. Together, they crossed to stand near Beth.

"Are you okay?" Emma asked.

Beth nodded. "I will be, once the drug leaves my system. Please, don't worry about me."

She then shifted to look up at Vaughn. "Is Loghry dead? You have to make sure. It's very important." She glanced at Emma. "If the ghosts are here, ask them. They'll know."

Vaughn watched Emma turn toward the ghosts. She seemed to be communicating with them. Her resulting expression of horror told Vaughn what he needed to know.

Loghry had faked his death before. Why not now? "He's not dead, is he?"

She shook her head. "Becca says he isn't, but how is that possible?"

Vaughn opened himself up to the future, which showed him two things, the location of a weapon and Loghry rising as if from the dead.

He told Emma he'd be right back and headed down the opposite path. One of Dagen's men had died nearby, his sword beside him. He took the man's half-sword and returned quickly.

The women were holding each other as Loghry staggered to his feet, already recovering. Unbelievable.

Vaughn followed the snapshots, levitated and came up behind the wizard. Holding his sword with both hands, he drew his arms back and swung hard. He struck the base of Loghry's neck and decapitated him. Both parts of the wizard fell to the dirt.

The women pressed their faces into each other's shoulders.

Vaughn was breathing hard. Fury engulfed him for a long, difficult moment as he stared at the headless body, enraged by all that Loghry had done through the years.

It took him a few minutes to recover himself. He labored through a series of deep breaths, easing his anger down. Loghry was dead and Emma and Beth were safe.

Together, all three of them had done a lot of good. They'd not only saved the girls in the cage tonight, but all the ones Loghry would have gone after in the future. If the wizard had survived, there would have been hundreds more.

When he'd grown calmer, he moved back to Emma and Beth. "You two okay?"

They both nodded, but each face was pale.

"Sorry this was so messy."

Emma rose to her feet. "It was the right thing to do. Maybe even the only thing you could do."

Beth stood up as well. "Thank God, it's over. There's no way he can come back to life now."

Emma placed her hand on Vaughn's arm. "I just spoke with Becca. He really is dead now."

Vaughn turned to Emma and slid his arm around her shoulders. He drew her close. "We did it, Em."

Tears filled her eyes as she nodded. "With Beth's help, yes we did."

Vaughn opened his free arm to Beth. She arranged herself next to him, leaning against his shoulder. He held her tight as well.

They'd done it. The wizard was dead.

~ ~ ~

Emma savored the close connection to Vaughn as she watched the triplets. All three girls remained hovering near Loghry. They seemed to be waiting for something, perhaps for his spirit to leave his body.

Vaughn leaned close and spoke in a low voice. "What's going on with them?"

Emma shook her head. "I don't know. Maybe they want to face the man who took their lives."

"Can he hurt the girls at this point?"

"I don't think so. I think this is something else."

To Emma's surprise, more ghosts began to arrive in the small space. Each was a teenage girl, no doubt victims like Becca and her sisters.

And they kept coming, on and on, silent and grim, their mist-like bodies overlapping one another.

"Vaughn, can you see the other ghosts? There are hundreds of them."

"They have to be the girls Loghry killed over the years."

Movement from the wizard's body drew Emma's attention. She watched as a confused spirit emerged, hunched and grotesque-looking. He glanced at all the faces and snarled, but none of the teens moved.

Near his body, a fiery red archway appeared. Loghry turned toward it and his snarls ceased. His spirit grew agitated and as the archway began to draw him in, he started to scream. Though he attempted to fight back, the power that had hold of him sucked him through the arch. He disappeared into a black abyss, the last of his screams echoing through the labyrinth.

Once he was gone, the arch vanished as well.

Silence followed.

Then, after a full minute, everything changed.

Emma found it difficult to explain the sensation that flooded the space, as though the labyrinth had been weighed down with a physical oppression, which no longer existed. Her heart felt light, and she was completely at peace.

The spirits of the girls began to celebrate. They gave what sounded like shouts of triumph at first. Then one after the other, the young women broke into a celestial, otherworld song.

Tears burst from Emma's eyes. *Vaughn, can you hear them?*

Like angels singing.

It is.

Beth leaned her head against the well of Vaughn's shoulder. She was shaking again so Emma put her hand on Beth's forehead and let her healing flow.

"Oh, that feels wonderful. Almost as wonderful as hearing the angels sing."

Emma glanced at her. "Can you see the spirits, Beth?"

"No. I can only hear their song. Wait, is that my name? Are they singing about me?"

"Yes." Emma smiled through her tears. "They're singing your praises, and I think they'll be singing for a long time to come."

Beth smiled. "I hear your name, too, and Vaughn's, just as it should be."

Emma was overwhelmed with the waves of gratitude that poured through the girls' voices. She had no doubt the sound of all these combined voices, raised in celebration and thanksgiving, would forge her determination to do good in her world for years to come.

~ ~ ~

As Vaughn listened to the ghostly singing with an arm around Beth and Emma, his entire Five Bridges experience slipped through his head. What had been nothing but despair had transformed into an understanding of what this new world could be. From the beginning, he'd fought his *alter* experience, believing it could never be more than a struggle for survival.

Tonight, all that had changed.

He kissed the top of Beth's head, then turned to Emma and dipped low to kiss her on the lips.

An ocean of love had arrived in his life, and he would never again be the same.

The spirits continued to sing, though they slowly began to vanish, one at a time, until only the triplets remained, three lovely brown-haired girls, each expression enrapt.

While Emma talked to them, Vaughn contacted Brannick telepathically to let him know what had happened and to ask him to bring in a search party to go room by room through the mansion. Brannick told him he would contact Connor, who was a Trib officer and who would know which of the uncorrupt TPS force he could ask to help with the search. Vaughn suggested they bring in a couple of trained police dogs as well.

Vaughn didn't have high expectations about what would happen. No doubt as soon as Donaldson learned that Loghry was dead, he'd contact the cartels, and in turn oust Brannick and Connor from Loghry's home. The best they could hope for was to discover if any other prisoners were on the grounds, then to release them before they could be taken somewhere else and funneled back into the sex trafficking underworld of Five Bridges.

Within fifteen minutes, Brannick and his team arrived, along with a pair of well-trained search-and-rescue dogs on the leash and ready to hunt. Every corner of the mansion was searched as well as two more hidden chambers within the labyrinth that Beth told them about. Loghry had been a deeply disturbed man and four more malnourished and tortured female vampires were found alive on the property. The dogs located at least a dozen corpses as well. No doubt more would be found over time.

Long past midnight, when word came that Donaldson was taking over the investigation, the team gathered near the guest house. Vaughn thanked Brannick and his men for their help. He shook hands with each of them.

As the team disbanded and headed their separate ways, he flew with Beth and Emma back to Emma's home. Emma prepared a quick meal of vegetable soup, sour dough toast and red wine.

His sister ate ravenously, being nothing but skin and bones beneath her ragged dress. Her shakes had stopped, at least for the moment, in no small part to Emma's intermittent healing touch. But withdrawal from any of the flame drugs was never simple and would require months to complete.

When dinner was over, Emma took Beth to the guest room where she would stay as long as she wanted. Beth was in good hands.

Vaughn, to his surprise, felt a strong need to be in Emma's spellroom. He made his way there and found both Toby and Stormy present, eyeing him curiously. The room felt familiar and comfortable as though he were coming home after a long difficult journey.

He'd never thought to have a woman in his life again, and he took a moment to silently give thanks.

When Emma entered the room, he opened his arms to her. She walked into them, then surrounded his waist and held him tight, her head pressed against his chest. "I can't believe all that happened. Vaughn, we made it."

"We did."

"And an evil man is dead."

"He is."

"And your sister is back."

He leaned away from her just enough so that she could tilt her head up and look at him. He smiled down at her. "And I have you to thank for all of this."

"I feel the same way. I wouldn't be here, with your arms around me, except that you helped me save those girls two months ago."

He caressed her face. "Emma, I could wait for weeks, even months to ask you this, but somehow this feels like the right moment and definitely the right place. You have come to mean everything to me, and I want to spend the rest of my life with you. Will you marry me?"

~ ~ ~

Emma would never have predicted that the night she fought and helped slay such a powerful wizard as Loghry, would end with a marriage proposal. It might not even strike the most romantic note. But with all that, it somehow seemed perfect.

She stroked Vaughn's face with the back of her fingers. "Of course I will. I love you, Vaughn. We're a team now, you and I."

He kissed her, a long lingering kiss, with his strong arms around her and his lips warm and full of tenderness.

The embrace only ended when a strange ghostly shouting had Vaughn pulling away from her. "What the hell was that?"

He turned her in the direction of the sideboard that held all her glass canisters, and there the triplets were, lifting the lids up and down and making what sounds they could from their ghostly voices.

Emma laughed. "They're celebrating our engagement."

Vaughn turned to her chuckling as well. "Love you, Em."

"Me, too."

He kissed her again, despite all the racket.

EPILOGUE

Three weeks later on a Saturday night, Emma sat outside with Vaughn and Beth. Vaughn had fired up the barbeque ready to cook some ribeyes, Emma had prepared potato salad and corn on the cob and Beth had made sangria.

Beth was staying with them indefinitely while she received intensive therapy from a good-hearted witch who specialized in long-term abuse situations. Having been imprisoned by Loghry for years would take time to overcome, as would the second-hand addiction to amethyst flame. The flame drugs were notorious for requiring extensive recovery periods.

As part of her healing process, Beth had taken a part-time job at the Tribunal, working the tip line for abducted teens.

Vaughn had quit the Crescent Border Patrol. Though Connor had wanted him to become a TPS officer, Vaughn felt compelled to go a different direction entirely.

Just a few days after Loghry's death, he'd presented Emma with the idea that together they could establish a safe house for human teens in Five Bridges. This would be a place where any teen, having escaped his or her captors, could come to seek shelter.

The organization would keep a high profile to make sure the word got out. Vaughn would also use his experience as a Border Patrol officer to provide round the clock security for an endeavor that was sure to enrage the unsavory elements in all five territories.

Emma knew it was the right thing to do. For the first week, she'd even hoped she could purchase Loghry's mansion to use as their safe house. But Donaldson blocked those efforts, and shortly afterward, it became the headquarters for a powerful cartel lieutenant.

One of the more positive repercussions of Loghry's death was that without his charismatic presence and dark wizard ability to control those around him, his organization disintegrated. Of course, others took over his clubs, and the places were back in business in a short period of time.

Fortunately, the new owners didn't have Loghry's taste and refused to offer up fresh teens to their patrons. In that sense, she knew she and Vaughn, with Beth's help, had disrupted a truly vile part of the Elegance Territory club scene.

After the meal, Emma had taken the leftover potato salad into the house, when the triplets suddenly arrived in a distressed state.

What is it, Becca? She put the salad in the fridge, then headed back to the living room where the girls flew around erratically.

The oldest of the girls by two minutes opened her mouth to speak, then rolled her eyes when nothing came out. She switched to telepathy. *My parents will be here soon, though you should send them away. I don't want to see them, none of us do. Emma, they've done something terrible. I mean really, really bad.*

What did they do? Emma knew Samantha and Davis. They were good people and Emma couldn't imagine what they might have done that could ever be characterized as 'terrible'.

You'll see. It's disgusting. We didn't want this to happen.

Becca's sisters nodded their heads vigorously.

Since events at Loghry's mansion, the girls had taken up residence in Shadow Territory and were working with a powerful dead-talker. The sage woman was training them to function as liaisons between the spirit world and the dead-talker community. In this way, they hoped to be of service to Five Bridges as well.

"Emma, what's going on?" Vaughn called from the patio. "Do you need me?"

Emma extended her senses, but the situation didn't feel dire at all. "No we're okay."

"Is that the doorbell?"

"Yes."

"Should I come to you?" Vaughn was always thinking in terms of security.

"No, we're good. Just enjoy your time with Beth. I'll let you know if I need you."

Emma crossed to the large entrance hall and reached for the front door. She had the oddest feeling.

When she pulled the door wide and saw Samantha and Davis standing on her front porch, she realized she wasn't looking at two humans at all. Instead, her *alter* witchness recognized at once that she was staring at a warlock and a dead-talker. "Oh, my God! What have you done?" No wonder Becca and her sisters were so upset.

Despite Emma's shock, she held the door wide, beckoning the couple to come in.

Samantha walked into the house with a fluidity of movement Emma often associated with those from the dead-talker territory of Shadow. "We've done the only thing that made sense to us once we learned of our daughters' deaths."

She closed the door, then glanced from mother to father. "You chose to take the *alter* serum? I can't believe it." She'd never been given a choice. But if she had, she would have preferred death rather than to undergo such a difficult transformation.

Each nodded solemnly. Davis took a deep breath. "We wanted to be near our girls, of course, though that's just part of it. We knew we couldn't continue our lives as they were in the human part of Phoenix. We wanted to be part of the healing of Five Bridges."

Emma remained staring at each of them for a long time. Her brain refused to make sense of the extraordinary decision these two people had made. She wished she'd known their intentions when she and Vaughn had paid them a visit following Loghry's death. "If I'd had any hint of what you were thinking, I would have argued this decision out of you both. I'm sorry, but I'm appalled."

Davis took Samantha's hand. She looked at him in turn and smiled a very sad smile.

Davis met Emma's gaze again. "We know the decision was unorthodox, and so far the girls refuse to speak to us because of it."

Samantha glanced around. "We were hoping they might be here. Their dead-talker muse won't help us connect with them. She's been emphatic that it must be their decision and we respect that."

Emma glanced toward the girls who had arranged themselves in and around the large chair Vaughn used almost exclusively in the living room. All three shook their heads in refusal.

She reverted her attention to Samantha. "Are you able to see your daughters at all?"

Samantha's shoulders rose and fell on a sigh. She shook her head. "No. I sense their presence and that they're very angry with us, but no, I'm unable to see or communicate with them. When you told me that you and Becca had talked to each other, I was hoping you'd be able to help."

Emma had no framework with which to deal with this kind of situation. She had a close working relationship with the triplets, but she understood the source of their anger. "I don't know what to tell you, Samantha, except to give them time. I'm in a state of shock myself over your choices. Ultimately, however, it will be up to your girls whether or not they draw close to you."

She could feel movement from the other room and wasn't surprised when the triplets slowly moved into the entrance area and lined up on either side of Emma. She also wanted to know their wishes in this situation. *Becca, what do you want me to do? I can send them away, but at some point you'll have to deal with them.*

I just think it's so sad that they did this to themselves and for what?

Emma took a moment to search for the right words. *I get that they want to be with their children. But like you, I question how wise their decision was. However, they've already transformed and I sense they intend to work hard here in Five Bridges, just as you and your sisters are doing, to help prevent this kind of tragedy again.*

Davis intruded. "Which of the girls are you communicating with?"

"Becca."

He frowned suddenly and covered his eyes. He gripped his lips together firmly, but his shoulders started to shake.

Becca cried out telepathically, *Dad, don't. Please don't cry.*

He looked up, his hand still in front of his face. He peered at Becca, now visible to him and drew in a sharp breath. "I heard you inside my head and you're wearing jeans." He wiped his eyes.

Emma was a little surprised that she'd heard Becca at the same time. Sharing in group telepathic conversations wasn't something that happened often in Five Bridges, perhaps another unexpected side effect of her relationship with Vaughn.

Becca smiled at her father. *It helps when people see us if we look something like we did when we were alive.*

"You're so beautiful, sweetheart." He took his wife's hand, glancing at her. "Can you see our Becca?"

Samantha nodded, tears streaming down her face.

But, Dad, why did you do it? Mom, we never wanted this for you.

Samantha drew close to Davis, still holding his hand. "Please try to understand. We had to. But it wasn't just your abduction that made up our minds. You know the family at the end of the street? Well, their oldest boy was given the vampire *alter* serum and now lives in Crescent. It's an epidemic here in Phoenix and in about every major city throughout the country. It must be stopped. Don't you see? We have to be part of the solution, especially since we're each convinced that if we'd gotten involved sooner, we'd still have our family."

Becca drew close to Davis first, and though a tangible physical embrace wasn't possible, she slid her ghostly fingers down his face.

His brows rose and he gasped. "I could feel your touch."

Becca nodded. *Sorry I can't do more or I'd hug you.*

When she did the same for Samantha, more tears followed.

Now that the ice was broken, Emma suggested the girls and their parents move into the living room. They had a lot to discuss, and no doubt a long conversation would follow.

Emma left them alone and headed back out to the patio. She shared the details with Vaughn and Beth.

Both were just as surprised as Emma that anyone, no matter how motivated, would choose to become an *alter* species. While their curious attention became fixed on events in the living room, Emma watched Vaughn with his sister. Beth had been able to see the triplets for a while now and took a lot of enjoyment in their presence.

Beth sat close to him, holding his hand. She had circles beneath her eyes from both prolonged second-hand drug use as well as from years of starvation. She would regain her full health eventually, but it wouldn't be a quick process.

When she released her brother's hand and leaned her head against his shoulder, Vaughn slid his arm around her, holding her tight.

Beth sighed. "Look how happy the mom is. It may not be the same, but she has her daughters back."

Vaughn nodded, his gaze also fixed to the odd family in the living room. He squeezed her shoulders and kissed the top of her head. His eyes misted over.

She knew how grateful he was to have Beth back.

Emma's heart swelled as she watched him. She loved Vaughn with every *altered* fiber of her being. He'd become the sun, moon and stars to her, the spin of the planets, the breadth of the galaxy.

He took her to bed often and spent hours making love to her. She couldn't believe he'd come into her life. She'd thought after Max's death she'd be alone forever. Nothing about the corrupt nature of Five Bridges life had given her a reason to believe anything approaching a normal relationship could exist.

But here was Vaughn and their sharing of their *alter* powers and abilities had become a promise of good things to come.

He met her gaze, his lips curving softly. *I love you, Emma.* Even his voice had a deep tenor within her mind.

I love you, too. Thank you, Vaughn, thank you for changing everything.

~ ~ ~

Even after three weeks, Vaughn still couldn't believe his good fortune. Together, he, Emma and Beth had defeated one of the most heinous monsters in Five Bridges, and they were all alive to tell about it.

Now he was here, held tight in the center of a family he'd never thought to have in Five Bridges. He had his sister back, and he loved Emma with all his heart.

Emma said he'd changed everything for her, but she'd done the same for him.

His gaze shifted to the triplets in the living room. The girls were lively now and fully engaged with their parents.

They, too, were a family.

He gave his sister another squeeze of her shoulders.

Beth leaned back to smile up at him. She even patted his cheek. "I should head out. I'm spending the day with my therapist, and right now I'm feeling the sun trying to crawl up my spine."

Beth spent most of her time in therapy, working hard to recover from years of imprisonment and torture in Loghry's labyrinth.

He glanced up at the sky, still dark and star-studded. But dawn wasn't far away, and he was feeling a creepy sensation through the vertebrae of his back as well.

When Beth rose to her feet, he joined her along with Emma. By then, the family in the living room had made their peace with each other and were also ready to leave.

He and Emma walked them all to the front entrance. He opened the door first, stepped outside and checked Emma's latest security spell. He wanted to make sure it was intact before anyone left the house. He was under no illusion that he and Emma were out of harm's way. Because of their safe house, they'd become targets of the sinister elements in the province. But Emma's spell held and seemed to grow more powerful every day. More than one spellcaster had remarked that even the dark coven witches and warlocks couldn't create this powerful a shield.

The evolving design had striations of gray which Emma said matched his eyes. He was part spellcaster now, sort of. He didn't make use of Emma's spellroom or her gift creating potions, but he could draw on her abilities almost at will. They'd become a very literal power couple, probably the thing Dagen had coveted in Emma all those years.

Vaughn spent part of each night practicing the unique spellcaster skills, just as Emma worked her levitation and her recently acquired ability to create a vampire cloak to shield herself from other spellcasters. She often used her teeth to bite into his neck and give him the thrill of vampire enthrallment. He was thinking he wanted to do that again, as in now.

With everyone gone, he closed the door, then took Emma's hand. She squeezed it in response. "Something on your mind, Vaughn?" How well she knew him.

He turned to her, released her hand and drew her into his arms. "You're a feast for me these days." He drew a lock of her long auburn hair, pulling it forward over her shoulder. "I love your hair, your beautiful green eyes, milky skin."

Her quirky smile arrived. "And what do you want to do tonight. I mean, exactly."

He smiled, something he was doing a lot lately. "I want your teeth in my throat like a vampire."

He watched a full-body shiver flow over her. "I love doing that to you." She cupped him low. "Should I do this at the same time, or would you rather I climbed on board and rode you for a while?"

For a moment, he couldn't speak. Both images sent desire hurtling to his groin.

When he could finally open his mouth, he said, "How about we do both?"

She gave a small cry, then threw her arms around his neck and kissed him. He lifted her off the ground, teasing her lips with his tongue until she opened for him. He thrust inside steadily until her body melted against his.

He had to draw back to see where he was going, especially since he decided to levitate and make it quick. "Time for bed, Emma."

"Oh, yes."

He flew swiftly to the bedroom and worked hard for the next

couple of hours to take her repeatedly to the heights of ecstasy. His ultimate goal, however, was to wear her out because he loved having her fall asleep in his arms.

He held her now, cradled against his side.

The sun had long since risen, taking over the world of Five Bridges. Mostly his world slept through the day and would rise at night to begin the cycle once more. But now he was with Emma and together they would fight to make Five Bridges a decent place to live.

Until the night called once more, he held her close, his heart beating as one with hers, his arms savoring each rise and fall of her chest against his. She was alive, and she was his. For the rest of his life, no matter how many days he was given to be with her, finding Emma would be his solace, now and forever.

Thank you for reading **AMETHYST FLAME**! Authors rely on readers more than ever to share the word. Here are some things you can do to help!

Stay connected through my newsletter! You'll always have the *latest releases and coolest contests*! Sign up here (http://www.carisroane.com/contact-2/)!

Leave a review! You've probably heard this a lot lately and wondered what the fuss is about. But reviews help your favorite authors to become visible to the digital reader. So, anytime you feel moved by a story, leave a short review at your favorite online retailer. And you don't have to be a blogger to do this, just a reader who loves books!

Enter my latest contest! I run contests all the time so be sure to check out my contest page today! Enter here (http://www.carisroane.com/contests/)!

Now Available 2015: Book 3 of the Flame Series - DARK FLAME:
Find it on my website
(http://www.carisroane.com/dark-flame-3/)

Now Available: EMBRACE THE HUNT, Book 8 of the Blood
Rose Series
A powerful vampire warrior. A beautiful fae of great ability. A war
that threatens to destroy their love for the second time...
EMBRACE THE HUNT: Find it on my website
(http://www.carisroane.com/8-embrace-the-hunt/)

Coming Soon EMBRACE THE POWER, the final installment of
the Blood Rose Series! Find it on my website
(http://www.carisroane.com/9-embrace-the-power/)

Also, be sure to check out the Blood Rose Tales – TRAPPED,
HUNGER, and SEDUCED -- shorter works set in the world of
the Blood Rose, for quick, satisfying reads.
BLOOD ROSE TALES BOX SET: Find it on my website (http://
www.carisroane.com/blood-rose-tales-box-set/)

LIST OF BOOKS

To read more about each one, check out my books page: http://
www.carisroane.com/books/

The Flame Series...

BLOOD FLAME
AMETHYST FLAME
DARK FLAME
AMBER FLAME

The Blood Rose Series...

BLOOD ROSE SERIES BOX SET, featuring Book #1
EMBRACE THE DARK, Book #2 EMBRACE THE MAGIC,
and Book #3 EMBRACE THE MYSTERY

EMBRACE THE DARK #1
EMBRACE THE MAGIC #2
EMBRACE THE MYSTERY #3
EMBRACE THE PASSION #4
EMBRACE THE NIGHT #5
EMBRACE THE WILD #6
EMBRACE THE WIND #7
EMBRACE THE HUNT #8

163

LOVE IN THE FORTRESS #8.1 (A companion book to
EMBRACE THE HUNT)
BLOOD ROSE TALES BOX SET

Guardians of Ascension Series...

VAMPIRE COLLECTION (Includes BRINK OF ETERNITY)
THE DARKENING
RAPTURE'S EDGE – 1 – AWAKENING
RAPTURE'S EDGE – 2 – VEILED

Amulet Series...

WICKED NIGHT/DARK NIGHT

ABOUT THE AUTHOR

Caris Roane is the New York Times bestselling author of thirty-two paranormal romance books. Writing as Valerie King, she has published fifty novels and novellas in Regency Romance. Caris lives in Phoenix, Arizona, loves gardening, enjoys the birds and lizards in her yard, but really doesn't like scorpions!

Find out more about Caris on her website!
(http://www.carisroane.com/)

YOU CAN FIND ME AT:

Website (http://www.carisroane.com/)
Blog (http://www.carisroane.com/journal/)
Facebook:
(https://www.facebook.com/pages/Caris-Roane/160868114986060)
Twitter (https://twitter.com/carisroane)
Newsletter (http://www.carisroane.com/contact-2/)

Author of:

Guardians of Ascension Series (http://www.carisroane.com/the-guardians-of-ascension-series/) – **Warriors of the Blood crave the breh-hedden**

Dawn of Ascension Series (http://www.carisroane.com/dawn-of-ascension-series/) – **Militia Warriors battle to save Second Earth**

Rapture's Edge Series (http://www.carisroane.com/raptures-edge/) **(Part of Guardians of Ascension)** – **Second earth warriors travel to Third to save three dimensions from a tyrant's heinous ambitions**

Blood Rose Series (http://www.carisroane.com/the-blood-rose-series/) – **Only a blood rose can fulfill a mastyr vampire's deepest needs**

Blood Rose Tales (http://www.carisroane.com/blood-rose-tales-series/) – **Short tales of mastyr vampires who hunger to be satisfied**

Men in Chains Series (http://www.carisroane.com/men-in-chains-series/) – **Vampires struggling to get free of their chains and save the world**

The Flame Series (http://www.carisroane.com/flame-series/) – **Vampires battle it out with witches for control of their world**

CPSIA information can be obtained
at www.ICGtesting.com
Printed in the USA
FSOW02n1258101116
27232FS